Welcome to Wolf Country

Welcome to Wolf Country

Doug Allyn

Five Star • Waterville, Maine

Five Star First Edition Mystery Series.

First Edition, Second Printing

Published in 2001 in conjunction with Tekno-Books and Ed Gorman.

Set in 11 pt. Plantin by Christina S. Huff.

Printed in the United States on permanent paper.

Library of Congress Cataloging-in-Publication Data

Allyn, Douglas.
    Welcome to wolf country / Doug Allyn.
      p. cm.—(Five Star first edition mystery series)
    ISBN 0-7862-3421-0 (hc : alk. paper)
    1. Private investigators—Michigan—Detroit—Fiction.
    2. Hispanic American men—Fiction. 3. Organized crime—
    Fiction. 4. Missing persons—Fiction. 5. Detroit (Mich.)—
    Fiction. I. Title. II. Series.
    PS3551.L49 W45 2001
    813'.54—dc21   2001033061

Welcome to Wolf Country

Prologue

I saw him yesterday in a Jiffy-Lube garage. First time in over twenty years.

Had my old Camaro in for a quick oil change, settled onto the teal Naugahyde bench to wait. Picked up a month-old *Newsweek* to pass the time and . . . there he was.

The headline read "The Mob Matures, the Changing Face of Syndicate in the New Millennium." His picture was splashed on the cover with a dozen others. Organized crime figures. I scanned the article but it didn't say much more. Only that he was a rising power in the Midwest— Chicago, Detroit, Toledo. Rich, ruthless, and nearly anonymous.

Seeing him in that group was quite a surprise. For openers, I was amazed he'd survived this long, and somehow managed to climb to the top.

When I first met him, he was muscle, nothing more. Just another murderous thug. Or so I thought.

But as I recall those days now, I realize that I underestimated him. Big time.

I think most people underestimated him in those days. A lot of them are dead now because they made the same mistake I did.

I'm one of the lucky ones. I've survived the years too, and

haven't done too badly for myself.

But it was different back in '85 when we were both starting out. Very different.

Chapter

One

At first glance, I thought they were lost. For one thing, they were both wearing business suits, and most of our clients are blue collar. Or no collar. For another, they were both white. We get a few white clients, mostly frantic suburbanites whose kids have been sucked into the rock-coke subculture around the Cass Corridor, but most of our clients are black, or beige, or variations thereof. So when the two neatly dressed types wandered in on a blustery November afternoon, I assumed they were out-of-towners who'd gotten muddled in the New Detroit urban renewal barricades, and stopped to ask for directions.

It was a logical guess. Wrong, but logical.

Cordell was banging away on the typewriter at the front desk, wearing his usual black turtleneck and jeans, looking like a recruiter for the Fruit of Islam. The larger of the two suits said something to him and Cordell nodded in my direction without looking up or missing a stroke.

They made their way cautiously back to my end of the narrow store-front office, the heavy-set one eyeing the stained ceiling and warped walnut paneling with open disapproval; the older aristocratic type stepping carefully, as though he was afraid something from the worn tweed carpet might adhere to his shoes.

I didn't get up, but I did take my feet off my desk. Business is business, after all.

"Are you Robert Cruz?" the heavy-set one asked. His white-sidewall brushcut and wary eyes contrasted badly with his slubbed-silk blue suit, which looked expensive but fit him poorly, as though he'd inherited it from a rich uncle. He had ex-cop written all over him.

"I'm Roberto Cruz," I said, rising and offering my hand. The ex-cop ignored it, but the aristocrat accepted it after a moment's hesitation. If he hadn't been so slender I'd have figured him for the rich uncle who'd donated the cop's suit. He was tall, well over six feet, with thinning silver hair, narrow, patrician features, and clear gray eyes that matched his immaculately tailored pearl-gray pinstripe.

"Mr. Cruz," the aristocrat said, "I'm Lester Bradleigh, of Bradleigh, Childreth and Osbourne, and this is my associate, Mr. Cobb."

"Gentlemen," I nodded, slouching back into my chair, "take a pew. What brings you down to the Corridor? In the market for urban blight?"

"Actually, Mr. Cruz, we've come specifically to see you," Bradleigh said, taking a small notebook from an inside pocket. "If you don't mind, I'd like to confirm a few preliminary details with you first. You are—Roberto Andrew Cruz, listed in your d.b.a. as partner and co-owner of Alma Investigations, this address?"

"That's right."

"The nameplate on your desk says Cordell Washington," Cobb said, frowning.

"The tall gentleman you spoke to when you came in is Mr. Washington," I said, "he's using my desk because his typewriter's on the blink. Now—?"

"Bear with me a moment please, Mr. Cruz," Bradleigh interjected, "you graduated from Laurance City High School, class of—'72. Are you from the Laurance area, Mr. Cruz?"

"I grew up there," I said, puzzled, "but if you're from the alumnus association . . ."

"Just one last item. Are you familiar with the town of Algoma?"

"Algoma? I guess that depends on how you define familiar. We ran track meets against them, so I've been there a few times, but not in years. Why?"

"You do know the area, though? Perhaps some of the people?"

"I know the area, or I used to. It was a long time ago."

"Still," he said thoughtfully, "you're the only—Mr. Cruz, we wish to retain your firm to handle a missing persons investigation. You personally, that is."

"In Algoma, you mean? You can't be serious. The place is only five or six blocks long."

"I'm aware of its size," Bradleigh said, "and it's quite probable the subjects are no longer there in any case. Still, we'd like you to look into the matter for us, and as expeditiously as possible. There's a flight from Detroit Metro to Laurance at ten-forty tomorrow morning, Mr. Cruz. We'd like you to be on it."

"Just like that," I said.

"Just like that," Bradleigh agreed. "I realize you may have other obligations," he continued, glancing pointedly around the office, his gaze resting for a moment on the sofa upholstered in fuzzy chartreuse blanket leaning against the wall, "and under the circumstances we're prepared to offer you a premium over and above your usual rates, which are . . . ?"

"Two hundred d—and fifty dollars a day," I said, "plus expenses, of course."

"Of ah, course," he said dryly. If he noticed my slip he was too polite to comment on it. "Would say, double your usual rates, a week guaranteed, in advance, be sufficient inducement for you to give our matter priority?"

"No," I said, "I don't think it would be."

"Really?" Bradleigh said, raising one eyebrow a quarter-inch, "I don't know that we'd be willing to go much higher."

"It's not the money, that part's fine. It's just that I'm slightly paranoid. Maybe it's the neighborhood, but when somebody offers me a lot of money up front for a job, I'm naturally curious about what that job is. Exactly."

"I assure you it's entirely legitimate," Bradleigh said stiffly, "as I said, it's a missing persons matter."

"Fine. Who's missing?"

"Before we go into that I'd like your assurance that our conversation will be confidential, whether you decide to accept our offer or not."

"Mr. Bradleigh," I sighed, "that goes with the territory, and I'm sorry you felt you had to ask. Now who do you want us to find?"

"Roland Costa, and his son, Roland Junior."

"I'll need a bit more information than that. Ages, physical—"

"The names aren't familiar to you?"

"Not offhand. Who are they?"

"Perhaps the name Charles Costa? The late Charles Costa?"

"Nope, I'm afraid that doesn't—" But suddenly it did. "Are you talking about Charlie Costa? The loan shark who washed up on Belle Isle a few weeks back? That Charles Costa?"

"Exactly," Bradleigh nodded, "that Charles Costa."

"And these other two? Relatives, or what?"

"Mr. Costa's brother and his nephew."

"I see. And you think they may have disappeared the same way?"

"Not at all. On the contrary, I think their disappearance is deliberate. We have no reason to suspect foul play, or at least, not at present."

"Even so, under the circumstances, shouldn't you talk to the police? Or have you?"

"Our, ah, client prefers not to involve the police just yet, and they tend to give missing persons a low priority in any case. We did, however, employ another firm to look into the matter earlier. Are you familiar with Kent, Farnsworth and Associates?"

"Sure. They've got their own floor in the Renaissance Center. We belong to all the same country clubs. I take it they didn't turn them up."

"Obviously not, but then the scope of their investigation was much more extensive than yours will be. It was, in effect, coast to coast. Farnsworth did cite difficulties in dealing with the local authorities in Algoma though, so I thought perhaps a second look there might be warranted, by someone more familiar with the locale. I don't expect miracles, Mr. Cruz. If you do manage to locate Mr. Costa, have him contact my office. But I doubt that you will. Basically, all I'm asking you to do is simply dot the *i*'s and cross the *t*'s on this, so we can put the matter behind us."

"Who's us, exactly? Are you representing the family?"

He looked at me oddly for a moment. "I'm afraid that's privileged, Mr. Cruz," he said at last. "Now, I hate to seem uncivil, but I must have your decision on this. I believe our offer is more than equitable, so. Do you want the job or not, Mr. Cruz?"

"Sure," I said, "absolutely."

"Good." He withdrew a manila envelope from an inside pocket and placed it on the desk. "This is a summary of Farnsworth's report with photographs and descriptions of Roland and Rol Junior, as well as some other odds and ends I thought might be pertinent. The details of the disappearance are straightforward. Essentially, they accompanied the body of Charles Costa to Algoma for burial, and . . . dropped out of sight directly afterward. If you have any questions, you may contact me at my office. And now if you'll excuse me, I have some calls to make. Mr. Cobb will conclude the financial arrangements. Good day to you, Mr. Cruz."

"It's been a—" But I was talking to his empty chair as he strode briskly toward our front door without a backward glance. No farewell handshake, no 'how's the little woman?' *Nada*.

Cobb shrugged and produced a checkbook. "Five hundred a day for six days, right?"

"Seven days," I said, "a week has seven days."

"Six days, seven days," he shrugged, filling out the check, "whatever. He's flushing the dough anyway, just goin' through the motions. But be damn sure you put in the seven days. We ain't the welfare office. He'll probably send somebody up there to check on you. Mr. Bradleigh doesn't mind spendin' bucks, but he gets what he pays for."

"We'll do our best."

"You'd better," he said, passing me the check, but holding on to it as I took it, his eyes locked on mine, "because if I have to come back to this dump to find out why you didn't, I'm gonna be very unhappy. Understand?"

"No problem," I said, plucking the check away and looking it over. "Have a nice day, Mr. Cobb. And by the way, how *is* the little woman?"

"Get stuffed," he said.

14

★ ★ ★ ★ ★

I escorted him out, not to be polite, but because I wondered what kind of wheels went with eight hundred dollar suits. I peered out through our flyspecked blinds and watched Cobb climb behind the wheel of a cream-colored Mercedes Benz 600 stretch limo. The car had already attracted a crowd of street kids who probably figured Smokey Robinson was in town. If our business had taken a few more minutes, Cobb would've driven away on the hubs.

I caught a glimpse of Bradleigh through the smoked glass of the rear passenger section. He was talking on a mobile phone, gesturing with his free hand to emphasize a point as though the movement could carry over the line. And maybe it could. For all I knew he had a video hookup back there.

"What was all that about?" Cordell asked quietly.

"Business," I said, waving the check at him, "missing persons, and I'm off to the bank before they change their minds. We just got well. Thirty five hundred bucks worth."

"Are you serious?" he said, frowning at me over the rims of his wire-framed granny glasses. "Who we supposed to kill?"

"Nobody. I have to fly up to Laurance tomorrow, rent a ride to Algoma, and put in a week on expenses scoutin' about."

"Where the hell's Algoma?"

"It's a wide spot in the road up north, about forty miles from my home town. The only problem I see is how to look busy for a week." I tossed the check at him and he snatched it in mid-air.

"Hey, for real, Bobby, what's the catch?"

"Beats me. It seems like there oughta be one, though, doesn't it. Or maybe we've just been working the Corridor too long. On the other hand, maybe we could invest a few bucks buying Mitch dinner and pick his brain a little. We owe him one anyway."

"More like two or three," Cordell said, handing me the check, "but count me out. I've got an exam tonight, and I've gotta be at Ford Rouge Three when the second shift gets out to talk to a dude about back child support."

"How much?"

"Twelve hundred. One twenty, our end."

"I thought we decided we weren't gonna do those anymore for less than a third."

"You're right. I got the old lady's number. Why don't you give her a jingle, tell her we gotta have our third. Course, you'll have to let it ring awhile. It's a pay phone at a 7-11 in the Parkside Project."

"Fine, fine. You want to get stomped for a yard and change, be my guest. I've got to make the bank. I'll give you a buzz in a couple of days to let you know how it's going." I pulled open the top drawer of the desk and grabbed my gloves.

"Yeah, you do that," Cordell said, still frowning, "and ah, look, you watch yourself up there, Bobby. Nobody lays out this kind of bread for fun and games. There's gotta be a catch to it someplace."

"Cordell, they're loaded, for cryin' out loud. They were driving a limo."

"I noticed. You figure they keep up the payments on it by givin' money away?"

I paused with my hand on the knob, seeing Bradleigh walk away without a backward glance, and the indifference in Cobb's eyes. "No," I said, "no, I don't suppose they do at that."

Chapter

Two

I stood just inside the doorway of Tufic's Green Line Grill waiting for my eyes to adjust to the dimness. The restaurant was packed, but then Tufic's is nearly always packed. It's the only eatery with a liquor license within easy walking distance of the Metro Central police station. The room has a comfortable ambiance, walls paneled in dark pine with sconces glowing red every few feet, heavy oak ceiling beams with hammered iron joints looming overhead, waitresses in miniskirts, net stockings and frilly red-checkered aprons scurrying between the tables, and above it all the constant clatter of dishes, conversation, and shouted orders from the kitchen at the rear. The menu leans heavily toward the beef-and-potatoes staples that cops favor, the fare's edible, the tablecloths get changed weekly, and the management furnishes modular phones at the tables on request, no charge. The place wouldn't rate more than a star or two from Triple-A, but Tufic probably sends more money home to Lebanon than the World Bank.

I spotted Mitch Zielinski sitting alone in a rear booth. He was hunched over, talking into a modular phone, his low brow furrowed, nodding as he listened. Business as usual. Since he made lieutenant four years ago and moved up to Metro Homicide, Mitch has become a twenty-four-hour-a-day grinder, hustling snitches, keeping hours that would burn out an insomniac, working out like he's in training for the Olympics, pulling stakeouts on his own time. Except for an occasional uptown call girl there aren't any women in his life that I know of, and no friends who aren't policemen, or old army buddies like Cordell. And me. Mitch'll make rank as long as promotions are granted on merit, but he'll never be an executive. He's got no more political skill than a gut-shot bear.

I worry sometimes about what his life will be like after he does his twenty-five or whatever, but not too often. It's hard to pity a man whose priorities are in order, whether you agree with them or not. Especially if you're in your mid three-o's and you're still trying to decide what you want to be when you grow up.

I made my way through the crush and slid into the booth. I picked up a menu and pretended to read it while I waited for Mitch to finish. He glanced up and nodded as I sat down, but otherwise ignored me, giving his total concentration to whoever was on the other end of the line. "Gotta go," he said, and hung up. I noticed he didn't ask about the little woman either.

"Bobby," he said, offering me his grizzly-sized paw, "you don't look too bad. Look like you dropped a few pounds, maybe. You guys starving to death down there?"

"We're surviving. The dinner's on us, by the way."

"It doesn't have to be, you know. Nobody's keeping score."

"It's not a free lunch," I said, "you can gouge those out of the civilians anytime. I need some background for a missing persons thing."

"Good," he said, showing uneven, stained teeth in what passed for a grin, "but it better be a prime rib's worth, 'cause that's what's on the way."

"It didn't occur to you that maybe I'm not in the mood for prime rib?"

"Nah, I know you two are livin' on Alpo and what you can root outa the dumpsters. That's what you get for quittin' the force. Besides, the rib's today's special. So how's school going?"

"I'm off this semester. It's Cordell's turn. He's doing really well, almost a four point."

"You know at the rate you two are goin' you're gonna graduate just in time to hang your diplomas in your room at the rest home."

"Maybe, but it takes a little longer to get an education than it does a diploma. We'll make it."

"Sure you will. All I'm saying is the job market's tough for senior citizens, you know? So what's this background information you need?"

"What can you give me about Charlie Costa, the loan shark?"

"Everything. It's Harry Fein's case but I've seen his reports. Charlie your skip, is he?"

The question was just a shade too innocent. Something had flickered in his eyes for a moment, slight, but I'd known Mitch too long to miss it. "No, he's not our skip. He's dead. And don't try to snow me, Zielinski, what's the problem?"

"Who's your client on this?"

"A Cadillac Square law firm, Bradleigh, Childreth and Osbourne."

"Jesus H. Christ," he said softly, "I thought I was kiddin' about rootin' through dumpsters. You guys musta really bottomed out. Did they hire you to waste Charlie's girlfriend? Or just to bird-dog her for 'em and then look the other way?"

I stared at him as though he'd started speaking Swahili. "Okay," I said slowly, "let's take this one step at a time. First, this is me you're talking to, remember? Your old buddy Bobby? I hardly ever waste ladies. Ask my ex-wife. Two, nobody hired us to look for a girl, and three, I don't have the vaguest idea of what you're talking about."

"You don't know who B.C. and O. are?"

"Why should I know who they are? The only people I know from Cadillac Square are muggers. We don't get a lot of clients with offices over there, or anywhere else for that matter. Look, Bradleigh hired us, me that is, to go upstate to see if I can get a line on Charlie's brother and nephew, and that's it. No girl, no roughing up little old ladies, zip. And it's your turn."

He pulled a pack of Marlboros out of his shirt pocket, shook one out and fired it up. He didn't offer me one, and I was glad he didn't. I still miss 'em when I'm edgy. And Mitch was making me very edgy.

"Okay," he said at last, "so maybe you haven't gone all the way in the toilet yet. Maybe you're just ignorant. I'll give you the benefit of the doubt."

"Thanks a bunch," I said.

A scrawny waitress materialized by our table, a cheery kid with acne, badly bleached hair, and a cast in one eye. "Ribs're on the way," she said, smiling, "would you care to order something from the bar, meantime?"

"Two Miller Lites," Mitch said, "and put 'em on my tab. The dinners, too."

"Back in a flash," she said, and disappeared into the crush.

"The dinner was supposed to be on me, Zielinski," I said evenly. "What's your problem?"

"You are, Bobby, or you're gonna be if you stick with this job. You're now officially a member of organized crime."

"What are you talking about?"

"I'm talking about your clients, B.C. and big O. They're

connected, all the way. All of their clients are either Delagarza family members or front corporations. The feds think Lester Bradleigh is Eladio Delagarza's *conseljal*, his number one advisor. You ah, have heard of Eladio, right?"

"Yeah," I said, feeling my appetite dwindling away, "the name is vaguely familiar."

"And you say Bradleigh hired you personally? You must be on the fast track. You got a pinkie ring on layaway down at Gulian's yet?"

"And this girl I'm not looking for? Who's she?"

"Cindy Stanek, Charlie Costa's longtime steady lady. Charlie was a mid-level soldier for the Delagarza family, a little loan-sharking, extortion, maybe an occasional kneecap or elbow job. His brother Roland is the mover in the family, not top management yet, but on his way, or at least he was until Charlie's girlfriend took a fall on a pissant coke bust, possession with intent, and decided to dump on the family for a deal. She knew a bunch too, a lot more than she should have. Old Charlie must've been into some heavy pillow talk, not too bright for a guy in his line of work. For awhile there it looked like we were gonna do Eladio some major damage."

"What happened?"

"She got spooked and took off. Got away from one of the D.A.'s flunkies in the Federal Building over on LaFayette. We thought at first they'd grabbed her, but it turns out they were looking for her as hard as we were. Then about a month ago, it all stops. Things go back to normal. No more hoods shaking things down looking for Cindy. And then Charlie turns up in the river, hands wired behind his back, two .22 mag hollowpoints behind his left ear. And they wanted him to turn up. If there's one thing these guys are good at it's making people disappear. Nobody knows what happened to the girl, but word on the street was that Roland dropped the hammer on Charlie himself and dumped the body where it'd be found to show Eladio he'd cleaned up Charlie's mess."

"Nice family."

"It wasn't personal. It was business. Besides, we ain't talking about Wally and The Beave here. Roland's probably aced an even dozen over the years, and from what I hear his son Rollie's a chip off the old block. Maybe it was cold, but Charlie was dead meat for talking to the girl anyway, and he could've died a lot messier if somebody else'd done him. Plus, it does show some style, you know? Icing your own brother. At least to those guys."

"So if Roland besmirched the family name by wasting his brother, why did he disappear? According to the report Bradleigh gave me, Roland and his son took Charlie up to Algoma to bury him, and then dropped out of sight."

"Can't help you there," Mitch frowned, shaking his head, "maybe they weren't sure Eladio'd be satisfied, though the way I heard it the old bastard was in hog heaven about it. But maybe Roland has a stash in Switzerland and didn't feel like taking the chance. What does Bradleigh want you to do if you turn them up?"

"Just have them contact his office. But I got the impression he doesn't really expect me to find anything. Just dot the *i*'s and cross the *t*'s, he said."

"Well, if they were really looking to hit 'em, I can't see 'em hiring you clowns, no offense. They would've kept their own people on it. Why *did* they pick you guys, anyway?"

"Algoma was apparently the last place anyone saw them, and I grew up about forty miles away, in Laurance."

"Forty miles is a long ways."

"Not up there it's not. It's the nearest town."

"How did they know you're from there?"

"I put it on my application form when I joined the mob," I

said. "How the hell do I know how they knew? Computers, I imagine, the same way everybody who sends me junk mail knows my shoe size and what kind of mustache wax I'd use if I had one."

"Yeah. Well, I don't suppose there's any harm in taking Bradleigh's money just to go have a look. Tell you what, though," he said, fishing a wad of photographs out of his coat pocket. He quickly riffled through them and dealt me one. "This is Charlie's girlfriend, Cindy Stanek. Keep the picture. If you turn up any trace of her, give me or the state boys a buzz, okay? You got any problem with that?"

"No," I said, "I guess I can do that." I looked at the photograph. "Nice looking lady."

"Yes, she is. Or was. Tell you the truth, it wouldn't bother me all that much if Bradleigh did hire you to waste those two. No loss, either one of 'em."

"Maybe I should call him back," I said, "offer him our group rate."

Mitch leaned back as our waitress deftly deposited two iced steins of beer on the table and bustled off again, leaving the scent of Woolworth's finest hanging in the air.

"Seriously, Bobby, maybe this particular gig's no problem, but the dinner's still on me, and if you figure on doing more business with those guys, you better find somebody else to bum beers from."

"Beer? You've got to be kidding. You think that when I'm a famous mob hit man I'll still be drinking beer? Somehow I don't think Lester Bradleigh hauls around a kegger of Blatz in the back of his Benz. No wonder you guys haven't nailed him."

"Beer's not the reason they're still running around loose. The problem is blood. Blood in, blood out. You've got to kill somebody to get into their organization, and the only way you leave is dead. That makes it a little rough to plant people on the inside, you know? You still all hot to join up?"

"I don't know. I used to work for an outfit that killed people. So did you."

"That was war. That was slightly different."

"Sure, Mitch," I said, sipping my beer, "sure it was."

Chapter

Three

The pilot of the Northways Commuter banked the six-passenger Cherokee sharply as he began his initial approach to the postage stamp airport fifteen hundred feet below. At first glance, the town seemed asleep as we passed over it, an enchanted village dreaming on the shore of Lake Michigan, surrounded by an endless army of hardwood forests clad in autumn uniforms of flame and gold.

I felt a catch in my throat, the phase-shift of time travel perhaps, a return to the past. It gradually faded as we made the final pass over the town, erased by the changes that were evident even from the air. The town had grown. There was new construction in the suburbs and a nearly completed shopping mall, its parking lot as busy as any in Detroit. Tom Wolfe was right, you can't go home again. And I wasn't sure I wanted to anyway.

The pilot taxied the Cherokee almost to the door of the thirty-by-thirty cinder block building that served as the airport terminal. There were only three other passengers, a couple of college kids with backpacks coming home early for the Thanksgiving break, and a salesman in a wrinkled overcoat carrying a frayed garment bag. He looked bushed and harassed, and I knew exactly how he felt. Our pilot was in uniform, a powder blue suit that clashed badly with his mop of

25

nearly orange hair. He was tall, freckled and much too young. And he was also the stewardess. As we filed down the Cherokee's ramp, he thanked each of us for flying Northways Commuter and suggested we wait in the terminal for our baggage.

But I didn't. As I stepped into the brisk November breeze I spotted an old friend, and walked over to say hello.

She was sitting alone on the runway sixty yards or so from the terminal, still wearing her Vietnam camouflage paint. A war surplus C-47, battered, dusty, a rime of frost on her windshield and grass growing up around her wheels through the broken tarmac.

I circled her slowly, looking her over, waiting to feel something. Affection? Fear? But nothing came. Maybe the setting was wrong, a chilly autumn afternoon at a tiny airport near my hometown. Or maybe it had just been too long.

"Interested in planes are you?" The young Northways pilot had followed me out from the terminal. We were alone on the runway with the lady in the camouflage makeup, and the wind.

"Not really," I said, "just this one, I guess."

"Why this one?" he asked, and I glanced at him curiously. There was an odd edge to his tone.

"Planes like this used to haul my outfit around," I said, "and I got my tail shot off in one of 'em. Why?"

"Just asking. Your name's Cruz, right? Didn't you play football here a few years back?"

"That's right. Tight end, but more than a few years ago. Should I know you?"

"No reason you should. I was in eighth grade the year you graduated, but I saw all the Wildcat home games and I thought I remembered you. My name's Jess Wright." We shook hands and I felt some of the tension ease. But not all of it.

"So what are you doing these days?" Wright asked.

"I'm a private detective," I said, smiling. I almost always

smile when I tell a stranger what I do. In a way it's like saying you grew up to be a cowboy. Or a fireman.

"No kidding?" he said, grinning back, "you mean like Mike Hammer and those guys?"

"Probably more like Amos Walker," I said, "but yeah, something like that."

"Who's—whatsisname, Walker?"

"It doesn't matter," I said. "You, ah, wouldn't be a part-time detective yourself, would you?"

"Me? No, why?"

"It just seems to me that you ask a lot more questions than the average airline pilot."

"Oh, that," he said sheepishly, "it's just this plane, is all. The cops asked me to keep track of anybody asking about it."

"Why? What about the plane?"

"She's a doper. Couple of guys flew her in last spring with Canadian registration, but if they were Canucks I'm Little Richard, you know? I think they were Cubans or something. Anyway, terminal regs require you to leave a key with the airport manager, in case of fire, but they pitched a fit about it and gave him so much static we got curious. So after they left we went out and opened her up. Three bales of weed. Prime stuff, the state cops said. Hundred and fifty grand worth, maybe more."

"Did they get the Cubans?"

"No way. The local cops staked out the airport, but they weren't real subtle about it, and this place is so small there's really nowhere to hide. If those guys ever did come back for the weed, they probably spotted the extra bozos in coveralls hangin' around the strip trying to look nonchalant and decided not to risk it."

"Funny, somehow I never thought of this neck of the woods as Miami North."

"It's not that bad," he said, "but we're only a twenty-minute hop from the Canadian border, and the country's so empty, you know? You could move an army through here and nobody'd notice unless they stopped in somewhere for lunch."

"I suppose you're right."

"It's funny how fast things change," he said, frowning. "Back when we were in school, you didn't hear much about drugs except in the movies, maybe. I mean, if some yoyo washed down a couple of No-Doz with a Pepsi we figured he was some kind of a dope addict. Hell, now high school kids are growing the stuff themselves. I figure it's gotta be TV. They just see too much crap on TV. What do you think?"

"I don't know," I shrugged, "but it sounds like Tom Wolfe was probably right."

"Who?"

I rented a three-year-old black Ford Mustang from the airport manager, a decrepit old codger who looked like Pa Kettle in a green eyeshade. "What with the deer season and all you're lucky I got this one," he said affably. "Got no idea what the next guy's gonna do. Have to hitchhike, I guess. Course, if she's a pretty young thing, I might just give'r a ride myself. Get it? Give'r a ride myself?"

I said I got it, thinking a smile from a pretty young thing would probably put him in intensive care, but we all have our little fantasies. Cordell and I have been trying to grub a living out of ours for the better part of four years now, so I wasn't inclined to throw stones at the old man's glass house. Whatever gets you through the night. Or the life.

In the parking lot it was time for a major decision. I tossed my suitcase in the Mustang's trunk, laid my carry-on bag on the passenger's seat, and then walked slowly around the car, looking over the pine forest at the edge of the tiny airfield, breathing air so clean I could actually taste it. No diesel fumes, no grit, no trace of baking auto paint carried on the wind from the down-river plants. No Detroit. I was only four miles from my hometown.

I leaned against the sedan, folded my arms and closed my eyes, feeling the pale November sun on my face, drinking in the air and the silence, with images flickering in the warm red glow inside my eyelids. Juking around the end zone after snatching a forty-four yard touchdown pass from between two Marquette High defenders, long summer evenings patiently working Bondo body-putty into the rusty wounds of my first Chevrolet with WLS Chicago blaring car-pulsing-rock in the background, my honey-haired date at the senior prom, her pale shoulders wreathed in white organdy, nestled in my arms in the school gym as we danced to what was easily the worst band in the civilized world . . .

I wondered how much of that still existed one right-hand turn on the highway away. I was on a low-priority no-sweat assignment, all expenses paid, with a week to kill and some extra cash in my pocket.

Four miles away. And nearly fifteen years.

I'm not sure what clinched it for me, but I climbed into the Mustang and fired it up, and when I came to the intersection on M-26, I turned left and headed northeast toward Algoma, thirty-six miles away, according to the sign.

I had no family to visit in Laurance, or anyone else in particular that I wanted to see. Still I'd probably know a few people there. Maybe it was the idea of coming back with nothing in my life settled or accomplished that bothered me. Just another clown living out a second-rate daydream, a kid's dream really, and jogging hard trying to outrun middle age.

Or maybe I wouldn't recognize anyone at all, and I'd wander the streets like my own ghost.

In any case, I headed northeast. And I should have felt terrific, rocketing down an empty two-lane road through rolling, open country, forested slopes covered with hardwoods and pine rising to the foothills of the Ojibwa Mountains to the north, on a clear, golden November afternoon.

But somehow I couldn't shake the thought that I was running away from something rather than toward it. That I'd turned left, not out of a sense of duty or whatever, but because down deep, I was afraid to look back.

Chapter

Four

WELCOME TO WOLF COUNTRY, the sign said. YOU ARE
ENTERING ALGOMA, MICHIGAN, HOME OF THE OJIBWA
COUNTY WOLVES, STATE HOCKEY CHAMPIONS, CLASS D,
1982, '83, '8— I couldn't be sure how many years the Algoma
hockey dynasty'd reigned. The rest of the sign was missing,
torn away by a shotgun blast.

Murdered road signs aren't unusual at this end of the
state, especially in mid-November. Over a million hunters lay
siege to the North Country during the firearms deer season.
They kill a hundred thousand-plus deer, seven or eight million beers, a cow or two, and a fair number of highway signs.
And sometimes they kill each other.

The town was much as I remembered it, but smaller—a
single paved street lined with store-front curio shops, a drug
and auto parts store, a five-and-dime with a poster taped in
the front window that said hot sand/coffee, an intriguing idea
if not all that appetizing, a supermarket at one end of town
and an eight-pump Shell self-serve gas station at the other.
Like most northern Michigan towns it had probably been a
lumber camp once. God only knew what kept its economy
afloat now.

I found the Ojibwa County Sheriff's office without any
trouble. It was just beyond the gas station at the city limits, a

single-story brick building that had apparently been a farm implement dealership at one time. A few pieces of rusting machinery were scattered in the weeds out back, and the plywood Sheriff's Department sign had simply been nailed over a faded, much larger sign that still said Allis Chalmers. Maybe it hadn't done enough trade to survive in the farm implement business, but it looked like the police business was booming.

Two black-and-white sheriff's patrol cars and an emergency rescue van were parked in the lot next to the building, along with a half-dozen civilian cars. A midnight-blue State Police cruiser was backing out as I drove up, and I parked the Mustang in the vacant slot.

I climbed out slowly, stretching to limber up. The drive from the airport had taken less than an hour, but it had been tense, for reasons that had nothing to do with the road. One of the county black-and-whites had the carcass of a six-point buck lashed across its trunk and I stopped for a moment to check it out, wondering what it was doing on a patrol car.

It was a fresh kill, the blood from its body cavity was still steaming as it dripped slowly onto the gravel. It looked like any other carcass, glaze-eyed, tongue lolling, with a quarter-sized bullet hole through its shoulder. Deer are beautiful in the wild, magnificent, but once the spirit's fled they're meat. Nothing more. Or at least that's what I used to tell myself.

I saw a lot of deer, alive and dead, when I was growing up. Hunting is a part of the culture of the north, a normal, acceptable activity even in what passes for polite society, and I happened to be good at it. I took my first buck when I was fourteen, two years before I could legally hunt alone, doubly alert for deer and the D.N.R. game wardens. I took nearly a dozen more before I was eighteen. And the year after that I was trying very hard not to be somebody else's trophy. And I haven't felt the urge to hunt since. Or at least not for deer.

The Sheriff's office was set up in what used to be the dealership's showroom, an open area that had probably held gleaming new tractors once. The room was painted off-white from floor to ceiling now, and the tractors had been replaced with a half-dozen battleship gray metal desks.

Two paramedics in dark blue uniforms were standing near the oil stove in one corner of the room sipping coffee and making conversation with a rangy deputy sheriff. An elderly woman with blue-tinted hair and a puckered mouth, wearing rhinestone-encrusted horn-rims and a bright green reindeer-patterned sweater was typing dourly away at one of the desks.

A blocky, hard-eyed Indian woman wearing a red and black saddle-blanket coat over baggy black trousers, with a black scarf knotted tightly under her chin, was huddled on a wooden bench against the back wall with a teenage boy. She was holding his hands tightly in hers. The kid's hair was a tousled dark jumble. He was wearing a blaze-orange hunting suit two sizes too big for him and a blank, dazed expression that had no more life in it than the deer stiffening outside in the parking lot.

The sheriff was sitting at an olive drab metal desk near the center of the room. He was holding a telephone in his fist and gulping coffee from a chipped cup as he listened to whoever was on the other end of the line. He was heavily built with thick, gnarled hands, rounded shoulders and shaggy, steel-gray hair that hung down in his eyes and curled over his collar. He was probably in his mid fifties, but he looked younger, with the open, eternally boyish face of a beer commercial jock. He was wearing a chocolate brown, fur-collared jacket of shiny, sateen material that somehow always looks brand new. The nametag on his jacket said LeClair. He glanced up at me, frowned, and covered the mouthpiece.

33

"Something I can do for you?"

"My name's Cruz" I said, showing him my license, "when you've got a minute I'd—"

"Okay," he nodded, "hold on, I'll be right with ya. Look, Sonya," he yelled at the phone, "I'm not gonna hold the kid, in fact we're gonna be movin' him outa here in about five minutes, and I've got somebody else waiting. If you can get a mini-cam here in the next half-hour I'll give you a statement, but after that I can't promise, okay? Right. Same to you, sugar." He banged the phone down, and brushed his hair back out of his eyes with his fingertips. His eyes were a light, almost transparent blue. They were red-rimmed and he looked exhausted.

"Now, Cruz, is it?" he said, looking up at me. I nodded. "All right, Mr. Cruz, I can tell you up front, they're not here."

"I haven't told you what I want yet," I said mildly.

"Algoma's a small town, Mr. Cruz. Your license says Detroit, so I gotta guess you're here about Roland Costa and his son, since the only thing anybody from Motown wants to talk to me about is them. If I need help on a hot car or a runaway, nobody down there gives me the time of day. Anyway, they're not here. They were in town a few weeks back to bury Charlie, and I haven't seen 'em since."

"Not surprising," I said, easing down cautiously on the metal office chair facing him, "no one else has either."

"So they tell me," he said, "on the other hand, that's not uncommon for people in their line of work, is it?"

"I suppose not. Did you see them when they were here?"

"Couldn't hardly miss 'em. They were driving a Lincoln limousine about half a block long, but I'll tell ya, Mr. Cruz, I'm afraid you've caught me at a bad time. We had a hunting accident this morning, and it's a mess."

"The Indian boy?" I said.

"Right," he sighed, "sixteen years old, dropped his first buck and his first man this morning. Dumb bad luck. The victim was trespassing, wasn't wearing any blaze-orange, stepped into the line of fire just as the kid there opened up. Took one six inches above his elbow and he may lose the arm. What's worse, the victim's white, and since we got the only bar and restaurant in thirty miles, the town's gonna start filling up with red suits and Bowie knives around suppertime and I wanna have the kid long gone by then. How long you gonna be in town?"

"I'm not really sure. Maybe a week."

"You got a place to stay yet?"

"No, I just got here."

"Okay, there's only one motel in town, the Windrift Inn, about a mile north of the city limits. It's right across the highway from Tubby's. Can't miss it. Now I'm not just givin' you the bum's rush here, understand? If you wanna talk, we can talk, but not now. Tell you what, you be here, say, ten o'clock tomorrow morning, I'll even buy the coffee. How's that sound?"

"Fine," I said, "I'll be here. But, ah, just so we understand each other, I've got an investigation to conduct, whether it happens to fit into your schedule or not."

"You can investigate all you want," he said evenly, "within legal limits, of course, but don't expect to turn over any rocks that haven't got somebody else's prints on 'em already. Between the state cops and that army of rent-a-dicks that was here awhile back, seems like Algoma's already been tromped over by everybody but the Canadian Mounties and the CIA. A word to the wise, Cruz. This ain't Detroit. This is my town. I've told you the Costas aren't here and they're not. Now there's always the off-chance you can get a line on 'em, but people up here ain't much on talkin' to strangers and they've already been pushed more than they care for, so you go easy, understand? Look, you're on an expense account, right? So enjoy your stay, see some scenery. People come up here to relax, you know? You oughta try it."

"I'll keep that in mind," I said, "tomorrow, ten o'clock. See you then." I rose to leave.

"Right," he nodded, "oh, and one other thing, Cruz. If you get homesick for the city, try hangin' around the super-market parking lot and sniffin' the exhaust fumes. It'll bring it all back." He gave me a bland smile that never reached his eyes. "You have a nice day now, you hear?"

In the parking lot, a small circle of hunters in various com-binations of blaze-orange coats, vests, and caps had gathered around the buck on the back of the patrol car. A fortyish blimp with a three-day stubble and a tiger-striped Aussie bush hat was lecturing the group about how important it is to read hoof splay when tracking a deer. He sounded knowl-edgeable enough, and some of the others were nodding sagely, but I doubted that any of them could tell a splayed hoofprint from a ballet slipper. Bush-hat was wearing a Bowie knife on his belt the size of a half-grown machete, the kind generally referred to as a hunting knife. The only problem being, properly field-dressing a deer requires deli-cate surgery inside the ribcage, and unless you want to leave a fingertip or two behind, you need a small, controllable blade, no more than three or four inches long. Ten-inch Bowies have their uses, for slicing pizza or fending off Viking raiders, but as a rule of thumb, the bigger the knife, the greener the woodsman.

I climbed into the Mustang, fired it up, and eased into the traffic. LeClair was right, the town was already filling up. I followed the flow north on the main drag for a mile or so.

Most of the cars began turning left into the parking lot of the town's only restaurant, a large, squat building with a phony fieldstone front and a flickering yellow neon sign above the door that read *Tubby's Tavern and Eats*. I turned right, into the parking lot of the Windrift Inn. And was pleasantly surprised.

Unlike the rest of the town, the motel looked new, neat, and thoughtfully assembled, two dozen units, each with its own tiled roof above naturally finished redwood siding. The court was laid out in the shape of a square-cornered U, with the motel office in the center of the base, and the open end facing the highway. I parked in front of the motel office and climbed out. The office window was a stained glass rendering of foam-crested waves beneath a pale moon. It should have looked camp, but somehow managed to look whimsical instead. A small neon sign on the door said vacancy, and I went in.

The motel office was airy and open, done in the same redwood as the building's exterior, which appeared multi-hued since the only light in the room was coming through the stained glass window. There was a dark leather sofa against one wall, a redwood counter, several doors, and a framed reproduction of Gainsborough's *The Honorable Mrs. Graham* keeping an eye on things from the corner. But except for the lady in the painting, whom I recognized from a 'whatcha mean I don't know nothin' about art' history course, the room was deserted.

"Anybody home?" I said, rapping on the counter. Nothing. I tried again. Still nothing. The door behind the counter was slightly ajar, and I could hear the canned laughter and babble of a TV game show from beyond it, so I walked around the counter and rapped on the door. "Hello?" I said, pushing it open a little further.

A lone woman was sitting in an easy chair in the motel's living quarters, wearing a bright turquoise bathrobe. I doubt she was aware of the TV flickering across the room. She was snoring like a sawmill and I could smell the reek of booze from five feet away.

"Hello," I said, "I wonder if you could . . ."

"Was there something you wanted?" a voice said sharply from behind me. I turned. A woman had stepped into the office, carrying an armload of sheets and pillowcases.

"I'm sorry," I said, "I knocked, nobody answered and I heard the TV."

"It's all right," she said briskly, depositing her burden on the leather sofa. "Did you want a room?"

"Yes," I said. I closed the door and stood aside to let her behind the counter. She was wearing faded jeans, walking boots, and a teal and gray sweatshirt. Her hair was rich auburn pulled back loosely in a ponytail that hung well below her shoulders. Her skin was the pale, almost transparent type that often accompanies reddish hair, lightly dusted with freckles. She wasn't wearing any makeup that I was aware of, and didn't need any. She was a very attractive woman, even in work clothes.

She flipped open the notebook on the counter and frowned at it. "How long will you be staying?"

"A week," I said, "more or less."

"You're lucky opening day was in the middle of the week. By the weekend we'll be full up. The rooms are fifty-two fifty a day, or a flat two fifty if you pay for five days in advance."

"The five days will be fine," I said, "do you take Master Card?"

"I'm afraid not," she said, glancing up at me for the first time. "We don't do enough year-around business to justify it. There's a bank machine next to the post office in the village

38

that will take it. Sorry." Her eyes made the difference. They were a deep, velvet brown, all the darker under her almost colorless brows. They transformed her finely boned features from interesting to very, very, interesting indeed.

"Is something the matter?" she said, mildly irritated.

"No, I, ah," I coughed. "I think I have enough cash." I fumbled my wallet out of my hip pocket and counted out five fifties. She riffled them, and deposited them in a cash drawer behind the counter.

"Would you sign in, please," she said, spinning the ledger on the counter to face me and handing me the desktop pen. I filled in the blanks for name, address, etcetera, and replaced the pen. "Cruz?" she said, reading my entry, "is that how you pronounce it?"

I nodded, trying not to stare.

"From Detroit? Are you here for the hunting, Mr. Cruz?"

"Something like that," I said. She glanced up at me again, then shrugged. "Come on, I'll show you to your room. I was just about to make it up."

She gathered the bundle of bed clothing from the sofa and I followed her out. She walked briskly to a cabin near the top of the U, facing the courtyard. It would have been pleasant to follow her all the way, but I stopped at the Mustang, unlocked the trunk, and got my suitcase and carry-on bag.

She already had the bed half-made when I stepped into the room with my bags. "Do you want me to leave the door open?" I asked.

"Not unless you're worried about your reputation," she said brusquely, pulling the sheets taut across the bed and tucking them under, "mine's safe enough, and there's no sense in heating the parking lot."

"Right," I said, closing the door behind me. "Sorry." I parked my suitcase on the arms of the leather recliner in the corner, a brother to the one in the office. The room was very nice, done in earth tones, beige walls, chocolate carpeting, even the obligatory painting above the dressing table showed more than casual taste.

I unzipped my carry-on bag and began hanging my shirts and spare sport coat in the closet near the door. There was something oddly intimate about the two of us at our separate tasks in the small room, and it touched emotions in me that had been sleeping a long time. I couldn't identify them specifically, but I wanted whatever it was to continue.

"Is this your first trip north, Mr. Cruz?"

"No," I said, "in fact, I grew up near here."

"Around here?" she said skeptically, "funny, the name doesn't ring a bell."

"Well, not *here,* exactly. Laurance. I was a Wildcat. Were you a Wolf?"

"Around here there's not much else you can be. When did you graduate?"

" '72. It was a vintage year."

"Possibly. But a little before my time." Her smile took the sting out of her words. It was a good smile, easy and honest. And very attractive. "You've been in Algoma before, then?"

"A few times. You know, out riding around with friends. And at the track meets."

"Really? What event?"

"Cross country," I said, "three mile."

"How did you do?" she said, plumping the pillow, and folding the bedcover over it.

"I almost always finished the same day," I said.

"Good for you," she smiled, glancing absently around the room. "Well, I guess that should take care of everything. I'm afraid the television only picks up two channels. The cable hasn't made it this far out yet. If you need towels or soap or whatever, just stop by the office. Somebody's usually there. And if no one is, next time try coming back later, okay?"

"Right," I said, "sorry about that."

"No problem," she said, "have a nice day, Mr. Cruz."

"Miss?"

She paused in the doorway.

"Look, ah, since there isn't anybody around to formally introduce us, hi, I'm Bobby Cruz." I held out my hand.

She glanced at it, then up at me, meeting my eyes. It was a very pleasant meeting, for me at least. "Sorry," she said, accepting my hand briefly, "I didn't mean to be rude. I'm Rachel Graham. Welcome to wolf country, Mr. Cruz. I hope you enjoy your visit."

"I hope so, too," I said.

Chapter

Five

I finished unpacking and then changed clothes, from my nearly-new blue traveling suit, to blue jeans, a well broken in dark blue L.L. Bean chamois shirt, and a pair of Alaskan Grizzly featherweight boots with cleat soles. They're the best walking boots I've ever owned, so of course the company went belly-up as soon as I'd bought a pair. Sometimes I wonder if the guy who concocted Murphy's Law was really kidding. Most days it seems as rock-solid to me as Newton's or Gresham's.

After a moment's consideration, I repacked my Beretta nine-millimeter compact automatic in the suitcase. I wouldn't need to wear it on this job, and I don't like leaving guns around unattended, in motel rooms or anywhere else. I slipped on my navy nylon windbreaker, carried the suitcase back out to the car, and locked it in the trunk.

I'd intended to jog across the highway for something to eat, but a glance at the jammed parking lot at Tubby's Tavern and Eats changed my mind. Hunting can be hungry business, and most sport hunters have the curious notion that deer take a siesta between ten and two-thirty, which is a convenient theory when you've been stomping through the underbrush since dawn and you're hungry enough to start gnawing the bark off stumps. On the other hand, since all but the most serious hunters would be out of the woods, now seemed like a good time to do a little hunting of my own.

I fired up the Mustang and drove back into Algoma. All of the parking spaces on the main street were filled, but I found an empty slot in the lot behind the five-and-dime and popped in.

The store belonged in a historical village somewhere, wooden floors and glass-top counters, light bulbs dangling from the ceiling on long cords, a giant metal cash register that went *ker-chunk* every time the moose-sized matron behind the counter rang up a sale. They apparently stocked everything from sledgehammers to safety pins. I picked out a blaze-orange canvas hunting vest, then followed my nose to the hot sand/coffee concession-stand near the front of the store. Two ladies from the high school athletic boosters were doing a brisk business in foil-wrapped sandwiches, coffee-to-go, and scarlet-and-black Algoma Wolves T-shirts. I bought one of each. When I paid for my vest I told the moose it was a pleasure to hear a cash register that went *ker-chunk* instead of beep beep.

"Beep beep?" she said, eyeing me warily. "What do you mean, beep beep?"

"It doesn't matter," I said, "have a nice day."

I drove out of the village, heading south on the main highway. According to Farnsworth's report, the brothers Costa, Roland and Charlie, owned several pieces of property in Ojibwa County; two vacant lots in the village itself, a two-hundred-acre hunting lodge in the foothills of the Ojibwa Mountains, and a beach house on Lake Onagon, a five-square-mile resort area southwest of Algoma. It's a good thing crime doesn't pay or I'd've needed a backpack just to tote the list of property they owned.

I glimpsed the lake several times before I got there. Algoma sits about halfway up an elongated slope that stretches from the lowlands around Lake Onagon to the broken, pine-covered peaks of the Ojibwas to the north. Each time the Ford topped one of the shallow, roller coaster rises on M-26, the lake would pop into view for a moment, glittering darkly in the autumn sunlight, encircled by golden aspen and flaming maple, its surface rippling in the breeze from the south.

A mile or so north of the lake, I turned onto the narrow access road that snaked down the face of a bluff to pass within a hundred yards of the lakeshore. I started seeing cottages in clearings on the beach side of the road, mostly tiny, rundown, summer shacks, with sagging roofs and walls wearing a hundred coats of peeling paint. A few were larger, though, with boat ramps jutting into the gray-green water, and some had small boats under tarpaulins next to the cottages, chained to ring bolts set in cement. A few of the houses had year-round mailboxes, but most had signs in the yards that identified the owners as summer people; The Lancasters, Harv and Ethel, Dearborn Heights, The Phillips, Dick and Mary, Montrose. I've never understood the rationale behind leaving those signs up all year unless it's to inform the local punks who rifle cottages in the off-season that the buildings are easy pickings, guaranteed unoccupied.

I read the names and house-numbers on the mailboxes carefully as I cruised down the lakeshore drive munching my hot sand., which was rare beef and delicious, but in the end I needn't have bothered. The beach house had a wide cobblestone driveway with twin fieldstone gateposts on either side that supported a wrought iron, full-width gate, and a sign overhead with eighteen-inch cast-iron letters bolted to three-inch pipe. COSTA, it said. Which is one of the things that I find appealing in this line of work, the sense of satisfaction you get when you crack a tough one. Spotting the telltale trace of lipstick on the cigarette in the murderee's ashtray, sniffing the faintest scent of perfume in the supposedly locked room, ferreting out the name in eighteen-inch cast-iron letters above the gate. Knowing that somewhere, Sherlock is probably shaking his head in reluctant admiration. Or something.

Unfortunately, I wasn't home free on this one yet. The grounds were surrounded with galvanized chain-link fencing six feet high, topped with loosely strung barbed wire. The gate was padlocked and Bradleigh hadn't bothered to include any keys with Farnsworth's report. Apparently he didn't feel keys were required to dot *i*'s and cross *t*'s, and maybe he was right, but in this trade ignorance isn't bliss. It can make you look stupid or get you killed, and I don't care for either option. Key or no key, I wanted a look inside that house.

I drove past the gate without slowing. I couldn't see much of the beach house. The lot was deep and the house was shielded by a stand of neatly trimmed pines.

The house next door to it was a mid-sized cottage, probably four rooms, with a rough-sawn cedar exterior. And it was occupied. A thin plume of smoke was rising from its chimney, and a green Chevy S-10 pickup truck was parked in the yard. Hunters, I guessed, using the place as a base to work the 60,000-acre Onagon state forest to the south.

I checked my watch. It was a little after three, so they were probably still in the woods. The pickup and the smoke might mean wives and kiddies, but I decided to chance that and take my shot, rather than waste the trip.

A half-mile past the Costa's drive, a dirt trail curved off to the right, and I swung the Mustang onto it, bumping and lurching along as the trail climbed up into the forest above the lakeshore drive. I followed it for several hundred yards before I found level ground beside the road wide enough to pull off. I parked under the fiery, overhanging branches of a red maple. If anyone saw the car, they'd probably figure it belonged to a slob hunter. God knows, there are enough of those, who'd hunt without worrying about the houses below.

I took my Bushnell mini-binoculars out of the glove box, slipped the carrying cord around my neck, and slid them into my shirt pocket. Then I stripped the wrapping off my new blaze-orange canvas vest and stuffed the vest inside my windbreaker.

It was a ten-minute jog along the fire trail to a spot that overlooked the Costa's beach house, roughly two hundred yards below down a gentle slope. I moved cautiously into the woods, the face of the bluff was covered with a carpet of leaves and pine needles and the footing was uncertain. And if I fell and broke a leg, I wouldn't even be able to shoot myself.

About forty yards down the slope I found a clearing that gave me a view of the house and grounds below. I knelt in the leaves, pulled out the mini-binocs and scanned the area. The small cottage to the left of the Costa's beach house looked abandoned for the season. The one on the right was still showing smoke, the pickup truck was still in the yard. And something else as well. A dog house. Terrific. It was facing away from me so I couldn't tell whether the dog was in residence or not. No help for it, but I wished I'd saved part of my hot sand. to feed to Rex or Fido, as an alternative for my butt.

I checked my watch. Four-thirty. Depending on how devoted the hunters from next door were, I should have at least an hour. I repocketed my binoculars and continued down the slope, keeping as much cover between myself and the occupied cottage as I could, but not ducking or weaving. Movement is what catches the eye, not color or shape, and a quick or unnatural move is doubly noticeable.

I stopped in the trees beside the road directly opposite the left corner of Costa's fence and eyeballed the situation. Still no activity on either side, so I trotted across the road and followed the fence toward the lakeshore, hoping to God the neighbors had boarded Ol' Shep with Aunt Minnie for the season.

As soon as the beach house shielded me from the cottage next door, I pulled the canvas vest from under my jacket, wrapped it around the barbed wire atop the fence, and scrambled over it. I retrieved the vest, then ducked into the manicured pines that surrounded the house.

The beach house was much larger than its neighbors and looked brand spanking new, a pre-fab structure, trucked in and assembled on the spot. It was two stories tall, with a gently sloping shingled roof. The walls were finished in hideous yellow aluminum siding with decorative brown shutters beside the windows. A brown brick chimney extended a good ten feet higher than the roof. The front door was in the middle of a full-width deck that faced the lakeshore, but I decided I'd better find my way inside somewhere else. I'd be too visible on that porch. But getting inside turned out to be easy anyway. Much too easy.

I slowly circled the back of the house looking for another door or an unlocked window, and I found one. Sort of. A rear bedroom window was open. Someone had slit the screen, smashed in the pane, then reached inside and opened it, simple as that. The question was, when? A month ago, a week, or say, twenty minutes or so. The month was out. Farnsworth's army had been through the place a couple of weeks ago and there was no mention of a smashed window in his report. That left a week. Or twenty minutes.

I checked the edge of the slit screen for rust, but it was

made of some sort of dark plastic netting. No help there. I listened by the window for a few minutes, but the wind and the lapping of the waves would have masked any sound quieter than a polka band and in the end, impatience got the better of me and I hoisted myself over the sill into the dimness of what was once a rear bedroom.

It was a complete shambles, the kind of total destruction only a tornado leaves behind. Or teenage punks. The chests of drawers were dumped, the mattresses slashed, the light fixtures ripped from the walls, and feathers from the torn pillows covered everything like new-fallen snow.

I moved warily down the hall to the bathroom. Trashed thoroughly also. The shower doors had been kicked in, leaving a tangle of shattered glass and mangled aluminum in the tub. Toothpaste and shaving cream clung to the walls like guano, and a roll of toilet paper'd been stuffed down the robin's-egg blue commode. There were stains on the tiles around the base where water had overflowed, but the floor was dry. I felt some of the tension in my shoulders ease a bit. Whoever had done this was long gone. Still, there was something about the savagery of the destruction that made me very uneasy.

The living room was even worse, or possibly it only seemed like it because it had been an especially handsome room once, a cathedral ceiling with natural wooden beams, a wall of floor-to-ceiling glass that gave a splendid view of the lake, a brownstone fireplace with a five-foot hearth. Trashed. Lamps smashed, couches and chairs dumped and slashed, they'd even ripped up part of the carpeting. Fuck and a few other obscenities had been spray-painted on the sand colored walls in harsh green metallic, but anyone wanting to make a search look like teenage vandalism would probably have thought of that. The paintings had been torn from the walls and destroyed, or at least most of them had been. One was still in place.

It was a small print of ducks rising over a marsh, but the vandals hadn't left it in place accidentally. It was bolted to a cupboard door set in the wall above the fireplace that concealed a small safe. They'd had a go at the safe, but with no luck. A hammer was sticking out of the wall a few feet away, apparently thrown in anger, and a screwdriver was on the floor nearby. They'd tried to pry the safe door open but only managed to scratch the paint and break the tip off the screwdriver.

And there went my vandalism-to-cover-a-search theory. The safe was a cheapo, and if they'd used the screwdriver to punch the lock instead of trying to pry the door open, they could have popped it like a crackerjack box. Kids? Probably. I couldn't see a pro passing up an easy safe in a house like this. Not when it was right there for the taking.

I stuck my head through the kitchen doorway, but didn't go in any farther. The refrigerator door was open, and everything in-it was now on the walls or the cupboards or the parquet floor, milk, bread, flour; it had congealed into a slimy mess covered with gray-green mold. It smelled like the Detroit River in mid-August, rank and foul. I'm no expert on mold, but I guessed it would take several days for the stuff to get this far along.

A flight of carpeted steps against the rear living room wall led to the upper level. I went up them two at a time and found myself at the end of a narrow hallway. Several doors opened off of it. And there were footprints, clear and white, against the blue plush of the carpet. Had the place already been dusted?

I knelt beside one of the prints. It was small, man's size seven or smaller, with the ridged, checkerboard pattern of tennis shoes. I pinched some of the powder between my fingertips and sniffed it. Talcum powder.

I moved down the hallway, keeping close to the wall to avoid smearing the footprints. There was a scent hanging in the air, familiar but . . .

The first bedroom had been mussed a bit, but only half-heartedly. Charlie's room, I guessed, from the photographs on the dressing table of a robust, barrel of a man, silver-maned, with a very photogenic blonde on his arm. Charlie and Cindy at Atlantic City, Charlie and Cindy on the Staten Island ferry, a group shot of Charlie, Cindy, Roland Sr. and his wife, and Roland Junior, arm in arm, standing in front of Caesar's Palace in Las Vegas. Everybody was smiling but Rol Jr., who would have been around twenty then, and looked bored with the whole thing. One big happy family. Only Charlie was dead now, and possibly Cindy, as well. And one thing was certain. The jerks who'd trashed this place had better hope the rest of them were, too.

I went through the dressers quickly, but found nothing of interest. Apparently they kept only knock-around clothing here and carried whatever else they needed with them. The clothing was all first rate, Eddie Bauer, L.L. Bean, which proved they had expensive taste, but I'd already gathered that.

I couldn't get into Roland Senior's room. It was the one with the spilled talcum in it. The scent was much stronger here, and I recognized it. English Leather cologne. A bottle of it had been smashed against the wall and the room reeked of the stuff. There were more photographs scattered about, apparently somebody was a camera buff. Most of them were of Roland, his wife, and son, but one was of Roland shaking hands with the mayor of Detroit. Not that there was anything sinister in that. Hizzoner's terrific at his job, which is getting elected, and he'd probably have his picture taken with Godzilla if lizards could vote.

Junior's room was more interesting. For one thing it had been more thoroughly ransacked than the others, bedcovers slashed, clothing strewn about. For another, it appeared that Rol Junior was more than a little strange.

Most of his clothing was paramilitary garb, camouflage shirts and jackets, several pairs of combat boots. Even his underwear was olive drab. There were pictures of him too, posing over dead deer like the lord of the jungle, but the most interesting shots weren't of Junior.

Pieces of a half-dozen magazines were scattered around the room, sado-masochism, heavy stuff. Blood and flagellation, young kids being sodomized by leather-clad fatsos in front of posters of holocaust death camps. Sick stuff, the kind that curdles your breakfast and makes you want to firebomb your local ACLU chapter. Nice fella, Rol Junior. A chip off the old block, Mitch said. I wondered if he'd helped his father deep-six his favorite uncle. A pity he didn't have pictures of that last little family gathering mixed in with the others.

I checked my watch. I'd been in here too long. Unless I wanted to risk meeting the neighboring hunters coming home from the hill, it was time to go.

I moved quickly back to the stairway, avoiding the spilled talcum, took the stairs three at a time and was halfway down the hall to the bedroom with the broken window before I gave up the struggle.

I just couldn't do it.

I couldn't pass up that safe. The house was demolished and the vandals had already had a go at it, which made it a freebie. I still feel a reluctant tingle of anticipation when I open envelopes that say 'you may already have won . . . ' And I don't pass up freebies.

51

I went back to the living room, rescued the hammer from its nest in the wall, centered the shaft of the screwdriver on the wall safe's lock, and hit it. Hard.

It was tougher than I'd expected. I had to hit it twice before the lock punched through. I jimmied the mechanism with the screwdriver and opened the door.

Not what you'd call a major haul. I found a loaded Smith and Wesson Airweight .38 with the serial numbers crudely filed off the butt, copies of the deeds to the beach house and the hunting lodge in the Ojibwas held jointly by Roland and Charlie, insurance policies for both properties, a key ring made of a brass plate with a series of numbers engraved on it that held a dozen-odd keys. And an envelope. With three hundred dollars inside. The petty cash fund. And that was it.

I ejected the cartridges from the .38 before I stuck it back in the safe. I hate leaving loaded guns around. I considered taking the cash, but I didn't. Maybe I was working for the wrong people this time out, but that didn't make me a member of the club. At least not yet. They say every man has his price, and maybe that's true. I'm not sure what mine is because nobody's ever made me a serious offer for my virtue. If someone does, I may sell, but I guess they'll have to bid more than three hundred bucks, because in the end I put the money back. But not the keys. I kept the key ring for future reference.

I reassembled the safe's lock well enough to pass a casual inspection, slipped down the hall and out the rear bedroom window and even managed to make it back to my car without being lynched by a mob of angry nimrods.

Good for me.

But all I'd learned from my career as a burglar was that teenage vandals are apparently a universal blight, that one of the people I was looking for was a lot nastier than I'd thought, and that I wouldn't sell out for three hundred bucks, which was some comfort, but not much.

Maybe crime really doesn't pay. Or at least not for everybody.

Chapter

Six

It was nearly six when I drove into Algoma. Traffic in the village had thinned a bit, but there were still groups of blaze-orange clad bravos who'd apparently spent their afternoon wandering the streets hunting for souvenirs. I didn't blame them. It gets cold and lonely out in the forest, crunching through shadowed glades with every 'crazed grizzlies ripped my flesh' illustration you've ever seen replaying in your memory, and only your shiny new umpty-caliber maple and steel miracle for comfort. Nervous business. Maybe when we all live in Megopolis it'll die out, but I doubt it.

Some people will stand in line for an hour to take a three-minute ride on a roller coaster. And some people will always hunt. One way or another.

As I passed the village limits heading north, I considered pulling into the motel office to ask for extra soap, or towels, or whatever, just for another look into Rachel Graham's eyes. Her impact on me had been a subtle thing, not like the proverbial bolt of lightning at all, but intense nonetheless. I couldn't seem to get the picture of her briskly straightening my room out of my mind. And I distrusted that.

In fact, like most men who've passed the big three-O without staying married, I distrust many of my feelings about women. It's a brave new liberated world out there, women are people now, with their own priorities, and as such, damn difficult to deal with. Without the catalyst of a mutual goal, i.e. marriage, my relationships these days are a tricky mix of chemistry, compatibility, and, as much as it grieves me to admit it, convenience. So when that old black magic suddenly makes my little heart go pitty pat, I wait to see if it'll slow, and it usually does. And when I find a woman especially attractive under suspiciously congenial circumstances, when she's offering me a job, say, or lying warm beside me in the blush of passion, or just confidently coping with domestic chores in my boudoir, I wonder whether the attraction is in the lady, or the situation. And I also wait. Because patience isn't just a virtue in my business, it's a survival trait. And because waiting, boring though it may be, is always easier than bleeding.

So I didn't turn right into the Windrift Inn and make up some dumb excuse to double-check my emotions. Instead I opted to answer the call of the empty tum and hoped it wasn't a sign that I'd finally crested The Hill.

The parking lot of Tubby's Tavern and Eats was every bit as jammed as it had been earlier, and I had to circle the building twice to find a spot. The place didn't look like much from the outside. It was an oblong cement block box painted battleship gray with a fieldstone front facing the highway. The interior, however, was a pleasant surprise. In more ways than one.

The room was very nicely done, long and open, with deep burgundy carpeting, round tables and captain's chairs of dark pine beneath ornately carved wooden chandeliers. A gleaming bar of natural oak stretched half the length of the room, and Naugahyde-upholstered booths lined the walls on both sides. There was a pool table at the rear with a Tiffany lamp above it, and a jukebox near it with Hank Williams Jr.

belting out "Family Tradition."

The room was nearly full, an odd mix of local civilians with wives and kiddies and downstate hunters, men and women alike clad in flannel shirts and suspenders, blaze-orange insulated pants and jackets, swapping war stories and jokes at a decibel level that turned Hank Junior's wailing into background music. And wafting through the haze and the din was the pungent, mouth-watering aroma of venison, a gourmand's delicacy in Detroit's finer dineries, but up here, thanks to the scarcity of game wardens, almost a staple food.

I fought down the urge to grab a plateful from the nearest table and carry it off to my cave. Instead I waited patiently beside the Please Wait to be Seated sign. And got drilled by those deep brown eyes again.

"Hi," Rachel Graham said, "would you like dinner, or would you rather wait for a place at the bar?"

I didn't say anything for a moment. She'd changed into a deceptively simple black dress with a modestly scooped neckline, and high heels. She'd darkened her eyebrows slightly and added a touch of color to her lips, and she looked like her own older sister. The knockout. She tapped her notepad impatiently with her eraser.

"You work here, too," I said.

"That's right," she agreed, "I work here, too, for now. Tubby's regular hostess quit on short notice and I'm helping out. Now, would you prefer a booth? Or the bar?"

"A booth, please."

"Follow me, please." We made our way through to a small booth near the bar and I slid in.

"Would you like to order now, or should I come back."

"Now is fine. What do you recommend?"

"The venison stew, the venison stew, or the venison stew."

"Gee," I said, "it's tough to decide. How's the venison stew?"

"Adequate," she said. "We have Molson's and Bud Lite on tap, and nearly everything else on hand."

"Molson's will be fine."

"Back in a jif," she said, and ambled off through the crowd. She looked every bit as attractive going away as she had up close. On the other hand, maybe she just represented food to an honest-to-God starving man. Maybe that's all it was. Right.

"You're Cruz, right? The detective?"

I looked up into neutral gray eyes beneath sandy brows, a skimpy blond mustache that didn't quite hide the cleft palate notch beneath the nose skewed at the base from the same defect, all assembled above an immaculate brown uniform, and topped off with a genu-wine Smokey the Bear cap. The deputy I'd seen earlier at the sheriff's office. He looked taller than I remembered, but then most people look bigger in uniforms. Or think they do.

"I'm Cruz," I said, "take a pew if you like."

He nodded and eased into the booth opposite me, took off his hat and placed it carefully on the seat beside him. It wasn't just the uniform. He was big. I'm just under six feet and he topped me by a good four inches and forty or fifty pounds.

"Buy you a beer, Mr. . . . Mattis?" I offered, reading his name off his tag.

"No, thanks," he said, glancing warily around the room, "I'm on duty."

"You're on duty in here?" I said.

"It's a dirty job, but somebody's gotta do it. You with that Farnsworth agency like the others?"

"No. With another agency. A smaller one."

"I didn't think you were one a those guys," he said, nodding in satisfaction, "but you're working for the same people, right?"

I let that pass. "How did you know I wasn't with Farnsworth?"

"Well, for one thing you got brains enough to change outa your three-piece suit to go stompin' around the woods. Saw your car out by the Costa's beach house earlier."

I let that pass too. "Did you talk to any of the Farnsworth people when they were here?"

"Talk to 'em? Not really. Mostly I just listened. They were from Detroit, you know. They mentioned that quite a bit. And they talked some about keeping outa their way or they'd have my job. Nice fellas. You want me to keep out of your way too?"

"Me? Nope. I'll take all the help I can get."

"Hello, Clint," Rachel Graham said, placing an iced mug of Molson's on a napkin in front of me, "would you like some coffee?"

"No, thanks," Mattis said, "I can't stay."

"I'm afraid your stew will be delayed a few minutes," she said to me, "Tubby's having trouble catching the deer. Five minutes or so, okay?"

"No problem," I said, but she was already moving through the crowd. I watched her go.

"Keep away from her," Mattis said quietly.

"What?" I said, glancing back at him.

"I believe you heard me all right."

"Why? She married? Or something?"

"I think she's got a husband somewhere, or an ex-husband, but that's not what I meant. She can be . . . trouble. I'm tellin' you for your own good."

"Is that some kind of a threat?" I asked.

"If it was a threat, pal, you wouldn't have to ask. It's just friendly advice."

"I can see why Farnsworth's people didn't have much use for your advice."

"Maybe so," he said, picking up his hat and sliding out of the booth, "but then they didn't find anything, either."

"According to the sheriff there's nothing to find," I said.

"That's right," he nodded, "there isn't. I'll see you around, Cruz."

"Yes," I said, "I expect you will."

He strode off through the dinner crowd, leaving a swath of silence in his wake that didn't dissipate until after he'd gone out the door. Uniforms tend to have that effect on people.

"Friend of yours?" Rachel said crisply, arranging a steaming platter of venison stew, hash browned potatoes and coleslaw in front of me.

"We just met," I said. "Friend of yours?"

"We've known each other since high school," she said, "I suppose he's a friend. Why?"

"He just told me to stay away from you."

"Did he?" she said, shaking her head ruefully, "he's not that good a friend. He had no right to say that."

"Good," I said, "why don't we do the Sugar Bowl after you get off tonight."

"The Sugar Bowl?"

"It's a nightclub just west of Laurance. You must have heard of it."

"I remember it very well," she said. "It went out of business six or seven years ago. Pity. It was a fun place."

"Ah, well," I said, "I guess I'm just a little out of touch. Any suggestions?"

"I'm afraid not," she said, arranging the silverware and napkin beside the platter.

"Look," I said, "I'm sorry if I seem pushy. If you'd rather not rock the boat—"

"It's not that," she said evenly, "Clint Mattis doesn't choose my friends for me, and neither does anyone else. But then, we're not friends, are we."

"Not yet," I conceded, "but that could be rectified. If you'd like to."

She stared at me a moment, really *seeing* me for the first time, and our eyes met in a glance of serious appraisal. Her gaze was as deep and intriguing as the forest at dusk.

"You, ah, said you ran cross-country for the Wildcats," she said. "Do you still run?"

"Sure," I said, "a little."

"Say, six miles? Three out and three back, rough country?"

"I think I can manage," I said. "How fast?"

"If you can't keep up," she smiled, "I'll leave you for the bears. Eight o'clock tomorrow morning all right? I usually run earlier, but not during hunting season."

"Eight will be fine," I said.

"Good. And for God's sake remember to wear something orange. Now if you'll excuse me, I'd better get back to work." She moved off through the crowd like a quarterback scrambling out of the backfield, but looking better than any quarterback I could recall. Although Greg Landry in his prime . . .

I attacked the venison stew with all the delicacy of a timber wolf tackling a caribou after a nine-mile chase. It tasted even better than I'd anticipated, if that was possible, rich and meaty, with greaseless gravy thick enough to float a spoon.

I finished the platter and pushed it away reluctantly. Only the thought of a six-mile run in the morning kept me from ordering seconds. And probably thirds. Rachel sent a waitress by with a second pilsner of Molson's without being asked, which proved her thoughtful as well as pretty. Or maybe I only thought so because she was plying me with alcohol. I think if I found Stevie Nicks in my bed, naked and dipped in raspberry jam, I'd probably wonder if she was *really* sexy, or if I just liked the way she sings "Rhiannon."

I spent the next hour at peace with the world, lounging in my booth, content, pleasantly stuffed, a cold ale at hand. A videotape of the Detroit Lions Monday night game was playing on the large TV screen above the bar, and I watched it in fits and snatches, but mostly I enjoyed a quiet evening at the zoo.

There may have been a serious hunter or two in the room, celebrating a successful day, but I doubted it. Most of these characters were up for the fun, guys who use the season as an excuse to skip shaving, slip into some funky orange duds and head north to whoopee for a week. They were a rude lot, rowdy and boisterous, playing cards or making less-than-subtle moves on the honky-tonk honeys at the bar. And far better they were in here than blundering around in the forest with high-powered rifles. God help anything they fell over in their present condition.

I even recognized a face or two. The blimp in the bush-hat who'd been lecturing on the finer points of tracking in the Sheriff's Department parking lot was at a large round table near the jukebox, surrounded by friends and a lot of empty beer pitchers. Several of the others at the table looked familiar as well. Apparently they were together, a hunting party, with the accent on the party half of the phrase.

By seven-thirty the room was too crowded to be amusing anymore as the die-hard nimrods swarmed in out of the forest, swelling the body count by half and the decibel level by at least two thirds. I'd waited, hoping for a chance to talk to Rachel again, but I was only catching glimpses of her through the crush now, and people were waiting for tables, so I decided to call it a day.

I managed to pay my tab after a shouted and mimed exchange with the eagle-beaked scarecrow of a bartender, who looked a bit harassed, but very cheery indeed as he took my money. I had a hunch he was probably Tubby. It would figure.

Outside, I hunched my shoulders involuntarily and zipped my windbreaker up to my chin. The temperature had tumbled into the thirties with the sunset, and vagrant snow crystals were drifting slowly out of the night sky, glistening in the yellow mercury vapor lamps of the parking lot.

My rented Ford was hopelessly blocked in, so I retrieved my orange canvas vest from the back seat, re-locked the car and abandoned it to its fate.

As I stood on the shoulder of the road, waiting for a break in traffic, I noticed a black-and-white Sheriff's Department cruiser parked fifty yards north along the highway. It was facing south, which gave Mattis, or whoever was in it, a clear view of Tubby's parking lot. It was also almost directly across from my motel room. Paranoia? Probably. But when you work out of a hole-in-the-wall office on the Cass Corridor, paranoia is a perfectly rational state of mind.

So I didn't go directly to my room. I jogged across the road to the opposite side of the U-shaped court, and circled around, keeping in the shadows. The motel cabins were apparently full now, and the parking lot was nearly as jammed as the one across the highway, a mixed bag of machinery ranging from a battered Chevette to a gleaming new Saxony red Cadillac Seville convertible. I caressed the Caddy's hood with my fingertips as I moved past. Maybe someday . . . but I knew that barring luck at the Lotto there was no chance.

Rides like a Seville convertible are never 'used cars.' They metamorphose directly from new to 'classic' with no stops in between. And the only way I'll ever own a classic is to hang on to my six-year old Camaro for another twenty. Which is a distinct possibility.

I slipped into my room without turning on a light, then stood in the darkened doorway for a moment watching the patrol car. It was too far away to tell who was behind the wheel, if anyone, and my binoculars were back in the Mustang's glove box. So I closed my drapes, shucked my jacket and boots, and flopped down on the bed to re-read Farnsworth's report.

And dreamed about green slime crawling slowly up the kitchen walls of a trashed beach house, and the anguished, agonized faces of young kids being sexually abused with posters of Auschwitz body stacks writhing and twisting in the background.

I awoke with a start, banging my skull on the headboard. There were voices shouting in the parking lot, and loud music. I checked my watch. Nearly midnight. I stumbled out of bed, rocking my head from side to side, trying to limber up my neck. I'd fallen asleep sitting up and I felt like I'd been slap dashed together by an autoworker on the Monday morning hangover shift.

The noise was coming from across the courtyard. Several cabin doors were open and their occupants had spilled into the parking lot, forming a crude ring around two clowns who were pummeling each other with drunken enthusiasm. And damned if one of them wasn't the hulk in the blaze-orange bush-hat. There goes the neighborhood. Bush-hat seemed to have the situation well in hand, slapping his opponent's wide, looping swings aside and digging solid body shots of his own. It was going to be a brief, painful encounter for the other guy.

I was turning away from the window when I saw Rachel Graham come out of the open cabin door beyond the scuffle, holding her blouse closed at the throat. Only it wasn't Rachel. One of the spectators made a grab at her as she passed, groping for her breasts. She turned toward me as she fended him off, and I caught the gleam of white skin beneath the open blouse, and got a much better look at her face. Definitely not Rachel. A much older woman who resembled her, with similar hair and build. From her unsteady gait I guessed she was the snoring lady I'd seen in the motel's living quarters the first day. Rachel's mother? Her assailant tumbled down and then I lost sight of her in the shadows.

The other scuffle ended at the same time, as bush-hat tagged his opponent with a shot to the solar plexus that dropped him to his knees. A drunken cheer went up as bush-hat juked around in his T-shirt with his hands clasped over his head while his buddy deposited his dinner on the blacktop. Somebody helped the poor devil to his feet and the show was over.

I stripped and took a warm shower to loosen up the kink in my neck. After toweling off, I pulled the blankets back and switched off the bedside lamp. But I didn't climb in.

Instead I padded to the room's other window, the one facing away from the courtyard, and opened the blinds. I could see absolutely nothing. I raised the window, feeling the icy rush of the night air on my skin. As my eyes adjusted, I could gradually discern the vague shapes of trees and bushes in the field behind the building. God, I'd forgotten how black the nights were up here. No city lights or smokestack glow to brighten the horizon. Not for a hundred miles to the south. Nothing to lighten the ebony sky but the occasional wink of a solitary star peeping down through the overcast. The Heart of the Night. Wolf Country. I wondered if there really were any wolves out there, slipping silently through the forest in the darkness. And I hoped that there were.

I closed the blinds, slid between clean sheets, and slept like a stone.

Chapter

Seven

I'd set my travel alarm for seven-thirty, but I was awake and up a good twenty minutes earlier. I shaved, brushed my teeth, then did ten minutes of stretching exercises to limber up, and fifty quick push-ups to pump up my pectorals, I hoped. Then I promptly erased any positive visual effect I might have had by climbing into my worn, gray-jersey running suit and down-at-the-heels Pumas.

At seven-fifty I heard a snuffling and scratching at my door, and then a sharp rap. I opened the door and Rachel Graham was there, her hair pulled back in an auburn braid, her finely boned face devoid of make-up, scrubbed and shining and looking like her own little sister again. She was wearing a black-and-red Algoma Wolves running suit, and she had two friends with her. Large canine friends, bounding around and snuffling at my legs, bright-eyed and eager to be off, a pair of Labrador Retrievers, with silky black fur and open, honest faces. Both dogs were wearing knitted blaze-orange sweaters, which reminded me. I grabbed my orange canvas vest and slipped it on.

"Hi," Rachel said, "ready to go?"

"All set," I said, "and good morning."

"Right. Would you mind wearing this?" she said, handing me a small canvas backpack, "I'm still a little sore from yesterday."

"No problem," I said, slipping the straps over my shoulders and snapping the elastic strap across my chest. The pack weighed almost nothing. She walked around behind me, fiddled with it for a moment, and suddenly a voice bellowed out of it, singing about detergent.

"You're taking a radio along?" I said, surprised.

"I know, I don't like it either, but we'll be running through the woods and we don't want to sound like deer. Do you want to loosen up at all?"

"I already have. Ready when you are."

And she was off without a word, at an easy pace at first. We jogged around behind the row of cabins and picked up a trail that led into the woods beyond. She glanced back several times to make sure I was keeping the pace without trouble, then nodded and lengthened her stride to a smooth, ground-eating lope. This was no Sunday afternoon once-around-the-block jogger. The girl could run. Fortunately her stride was enough shorter than mine that I could cruise along comfortably in her wake, which was a very pleasant place to cruise.

It was a beautiful morning for a run, mid-forties, the air crisp and clean, with a bite that brought color to your cheeks without searing your throat. We were following a trail that rose and fell through low, rolling hills, thick with flaming maple and yellow birch, our shoes crunching the fallen leaves underfoot. The dogs circled us as we ran, covering twice as much ground as we were, noses down, going airborne over obstacles with careless ease, beautifully conditioned animals in their prime having the time of their lives. And I knew exactly how they felt. Well, almost.

The only negative about the situation was that the trail was too narrow to allow conversation, not that I'm much on talking and running, but a word or two would have been nice.

And then, about twenty minutes and roughly three miles out, we broke into a clearing a hundred yards or so across, and I moved up to run alongside her.

"How are you doing?" she said, glancing up at me. Her eyes were sparkling in the morning sunlight, her skin gleaming with a faint sheen of perspiration.

"Fine," I said honestly, "just fine."

"Good," she said. "Are you, ah, good for an extra mile? I promise it'll be worth the effort."

"I've got an appointment in town at ten," I said.

"Well then," she said, glancing at her watch and then grinning wickedly up at me, "I guess we'd better get a move on, hadn't we?" And she broke into a sprint, covering the next fifty yards in a single sustained burst of speed, disappearing into the pines at the edge of the clearing with a twenty-five yard lead.

I didn't trust my legs enough to sprint, but I picked up the pace sufficiently to close the distance. There was something wild in that grin of hers, a primordial challenge, and I pounded along happily after her, keeping an eye peeled for saber-tooth tigers.

And then I was in the pines and it took all of my concentration just to keep from breaking my neck. The trail snaked up the face of a long, uneven slope, weaving between the shaded trunks of mature red pines nearly a hundred feet high, with broken boughs and slippery patches of pine needles underfoot. Rachel disappeared over the crest of the ridge ahead of me and I cursed silently and poured it on, pumping hard to catch up. It would be easy to lose her in this tangle and the idea of wandering around calling for help didn't appeal to me at all. But then I topped the ridge and broke into the sunlight, and slowed to a jog.

Rachel was twenty yards below me, pacing around the perimeter of a shelf on the eastern face of the ridge, shaking her arms to keep them loose and doing deep breathing. Beyond her was the roof of a birch forest spread out in the valley below, stretching off in the distance to the foothills of the Ojibwas to the north and east. White birches, their papery bark in stark contrast with the forest floor, upper branches gleaming like burnished copper in the clear morning light.

I walked the last few yards down the ridge face to the shelf, slipped the pack off my shoulders and parked it on a stump, and turned off the drone of the morning farm report. The dogs were sprawled a few yards off, panting and content.

"Well," Rachel said, turning to face me, arms akimbo, as I peeled off the blaze-orange vest and tossed it in the general direction of the pack, "what do you think?"

"Very nice," I said, "but couldn't you have picked a spot with a view?" And I placed my hands on her shoulders, bent down, and kissed her on the mouth. Her lips tasted salty and slick from the run, and very, very good. But we weren't children, and she looked up at me with guarded appraisal as I straightened.

"What was that for?"

"If I hadn't done that," I said honestly, "I think I would always have regretted not doing it."

"If that's a line," she said evenly, "it isn't bad."

"I don't have any lines," I said, "can't seem to remember 'em. Or jokes either, for that matter. Are we still friends?"

"If I chose my friends by the way they kiss we might be, but I don't." She resumed walking, but more slowly now, and I fell into place beside her. "I really don't know anything about you, you know. For instance, what do you do, Cruz? For a living, I mean."

"I'm a private detective," I said, "rental heat."

"You're kidding," she said, glancing up at me to see if I

was. At least she didn't laugh. "You mean like Spenser? On television?"

"I think he works out of a fire station in Boston," I said. "My partner and I work out of a store-front office on the Cass Corridor in Detroit. And we don't get many beautiful blonde customers. Unless they're guys wearing wigs."

"Why on earth would anybody want to work down there," she said seriously, "I mean, no offense, but isn't that, well, in the slums?"

"My partner's from the area, it's his home ground. And the rent's cheap. And I guess I like the action. And the work's always interesting."

"I can imagine," she said.

"Actually, you probably can't," I said, shaking my head ruefully, "sometimes I can't imagine it myself."

"But you said you ran for the Wildcats. Are you from around here? Laurance, I mean." She pronounced it Lo-ranhz, like a native.

"I grew up there. But I left when I was eighteen, and I've never been back."

"I don't understand that," she said frankly, "I don't see how anybody could live up here and not want to come back."

"Have you ever left?" I said, "ever been anyplace else?"

"Oh sure. I've been more places than you could keep track of without a calculator. My husband was a musician, and probably still is, for all I know. I traveled with him for . . . nearly four years, all over the country. I met him at the Sugar Bowl in fact, which is why it struck me oddly that you invited me there. I was sixteen and green as the grass . . . God, what a mess. But I'm home now. And I won't ever leave again, or at least, not for long. Don't you miss all this?" she said, indicating the scenery around us with a wave of her hand.

"Actually, I don't think I really did, until this trip. I've been gone a long time." I stopped at the edge of the shelf, looking out over the valley. The congregation of white birch below seemed to be swaying in ecstasy with the wind, praising the morning sun. "I guess I'd forgotten what it was like. Or maybe I didn't want to remember. I hope I won't regret making this trip."

"I hope you won't too," she said, leaning against my shoulder. She turned her face up toward mine and we kissed again, and much more thoroughly this time. I felt her move gently against me, felt the pressure of her breasts firm against my chest, the suppleness of her shoulders in my hands. And I was having breathing difficulties that had nothing to do with the run.

"Hey," she said softly, after a gentle century, "maybe we'd better save some energy for the trip ba— Oh! Damn, damn, damn! Max! Sit! Sit!" She pushed me away and grabbed the female lab by the collar. The male was holding a small rabbit in his jaws, slavering blood and drool on the ground, wild-eyed and wired up. The female was snapping at him, trying to snatch his kill. Grabbing her collar, Rachel hauled her bodily away, with the dog battling her every step of the way.

The rabbit struggled pitifully, trying to squirm free of Max's jaws. No luck. And then it began crying, wailing like a newborn baby.

"Oh my God," Rachel said, tears streaming down her face. "Drop it, Max. Damn you! Drop it!"

"You'll have to get the female away from here. He won't give it up while she's around. Go on, start back. We'll catch up."

"All right, all right, but hurry!" Fighting her tears, Rachel dragged the female off by her collar, leading her back into the woods. At the tree line, she let her go and I thought she might come charging back. She didn't. Rachel called her, and after a moment's hesitation, the female followed her over the ridge.

"Good dog, good boy, Max," I said, kneeling beside the dog, petting him, getting him used to my touch. I hoped. He was still quivering with excitement, eyeing me suspiciously.

"Good dog." After running my hands over his flanks a moment, I worked my fingers over his ears and his face, murmuring to him all the while. Hooking my thumb in the hinge of his jaw, I began tugging gently, forcing his mouth open. The moment of truth. If he growled or snapped at me now . . .

But he didn't. Instead, he gently placed the dying rabbit in my hand. Leaning away from him, I laid it on the leaves as far from us as I could reach, still holding Max by the collar.

Unfortunately, the rabbit wasn't quite dead. His shoulders and ribcage were crushed, but he was trying to escape by thrusting himself along with his hind legs. The movement excited the dog and he nearly jerked my arm out of its socket lunging at his prey.

"Sit, dammit!" I roared. He did, but he wouldn't for long. Clenching my teeth, I stamped on the rabbit, bringing the edge of my heel down at the base of its skull, tasting a rush of sour bile at the back of my throat as the bones crunched underfoot.

Easing my grip, I let Max move closer to sniff the carcass, feeling his tension ebb as he realized it was dead. Satisfied, he grinned up at me, his tail wagging, waiting for well-earned praise.

He was right. He'd scored. He'd won the game, home run, bottom of the ninth, dunked a bucket at the buzzer, KO'd the bunny in the twelfth round. I didn't feel much like giving him a high-five, but I couldn't really be angry with him either. He'd done what a hundred thousand years of hunting heritage told him to. Just a workin' stiff. Like me.

Gouging a quick trench in the leafy loam with my heel, I nudged the rabbit's body into it, then covered it again. Max eyed me suspiciously. What was this? Probably figured me for a weasel who'd sneak back later to steal his lunch. Which made him a fair judge of character.

I let Max sniff the bunny's grave, but his interest was already waning. This game was over. He'd won, the rabbit lost, end of story. And a very special morning.

When I let him go, Max circled the clearing once, looking for another score, then he turned and loped up the ridge, nose to the ground, trailing Rachel and the bitch. I slipped the backpack on without bothering to turn on the radio, and trotted after him into the trees.

Rachel and the female were waiting for us in the clearing on the far side of the ridge. Neither of us had much to say. She asked the question with her eyes, I nodded, and that was it.

We resumed the jog back to the motel, but it wasn't the joyful romp it had been on the way out. There was a thoughtful distance between us again. And blood on the heel of my running shoe.

We slowed in the broken, brushy field a hundred yards from the rear of the motel, and walked the rest of the way, breathing deeply and shrugging to keep loose. There was a chain-link kennel attached to the rear wall of the motel office, and the dogs bolted ahead and flopped down in front of it, panting.

"Thank you for helping out back there," Rachel said formally. "I'm sorry it happened, I ah . . . ."

"I'm sorry too," I said, "maybe we'll have better luck next time."

"Maybe," she sighed, "I don't know. I'm not much on luck."

"Can I buy you lunch?" I asked, "or supper? Or something?"

"I think I'd like that very much," she said, "and any other time I'd say yes. But I promised Tubby I'd help him out this week, and you've seen what it's like over there. I just don't know," she shrugged, "Can we play it by ear?"

"I guess we'll have to," I said. "Look, I hate to just jog and run, but I've got a ten o'clock appointment and I have to go. Thanks for a very . . . interesting morning. I'll see you later. Promise." And I offered her my hand. She glanced up at me, surprised, then smiled wanly and we shook on it.

"Whatever else may happen," I said, "we'll always have Paris."

"You know," she said, "you're more than slightly strange."

"Thank you," I nodded, "thank you very much."

Chapter

Eight

I showered quickly and changed into my blue suit, black loafers, and maize and blue striped tie. Ordinarily I'm a casual dresser. It's not prudent to look too prosperous when you work on the Corridor. But I had an appointment with a small-town sheriff, and cops make snap judgments about people on outward appearances. They've no other choice. And I was hoping to get some information, or help, or whatever. As long as it was free, of course.

I jogged across the highway to Tubby's. The Mustang was parked where I'd left it, looking a bit forlorn in the nearly empty lot. I checked it over out of habit, but nobody'd had a go at anything, so I climbed in, fired it up, and drove into Algoma.

But even as I drove I couldn't get the image of the rabbit and the dog out of my mind. I kept replaying it, shouting at the dog and wincing as I felt the bones crumple underfoot. And I decided that perhaps the incident wasn't the disaster I'd thought it was at first.

True, it had mangled a magic morning, but if that was all it took to trash a potential romance, then it was probably no loss. I'm a fatalist about relationships. They either work or they don't, and trying too hard to make them work is like swinging for the fences every time you're at bat. You're a lot more likely to strike out.

And there was a message for me in the crunching bones. I'd been seeing this town and possibly the girl as well through a rose-colored, nostalgic mist. And I'd forgotten what this country was really like. Beautiful? Absolutely. But fierce and unforgiving as well. I'd been sent up here to look for two very hard people. And in the forest, only the trees die of old age.

The Sheriff's Department parking lot was nearly deserted, no emergency rescue van, no State Police cars. And the office wasn't exactly excitement central either. The elderly lady in the rhinestone-encrusted horn-rims was working at her desk, wearing the same reindeer-patterned green sweater. LeClair was alone at his desk against the wall, gloomily scanning a report. His jacket was draped over the back of his chair, and his brown necktie was dangling carelessly beneath his open collar. He was sipping coffee from a chipped china mug with a star on it. He looked weary and harassed, like a class C coach during a losing season. My arrival didn't seem to brighten his outlook much.

"Cruz, right?" he sighed, glancing up as I pulled up a chair, "and what can the County of Ojibwa do for you today, Mr. Cruz?"

"You said we could talk today," I reminded him mildly, "about Roland Costa and son?"

"Ah, yes," he nodded, "I do recall saying something about that. It seems like a very long time ago. I had to deliver that Indian kid to his relatives in Marquette last night. Got back about four this morning. But what the hell. What did you want to talk about?"

"I'll take whatever you want to give me," I said, "I'm not proud."

He stared at me a moment without speaking. "Let me get this straight," he said at last, "you're *asking* me about the

Costas? Politely? Is that right?"

"I'd say that's a fair assessment," I said, puzzled, "Why?"

"Because Farnsworth's people didn't ask me doodly. They questioned the property owners along the lakeshore, none too politely, I might add, which brought in a raft of complaints. Then they drove all over the hunting lodge on quadra-trax, only they didn't know squat about the property lines up there, or didn't care, which brought in another load of complaints. And when I politely suggested they cool their enthusiasm a little, they told me I didn't have adequate resources here to conduct a proper search and demanded access to my files. And then they brought in a goddamn chopper, for chrissake, and landed it in the supermarket parking lot without so much as a by-your-leave, at which point I cited 'em as a public nuisance and a half-dozen other things, and ran 'em outa town. So if I'm not exactly falling all over myself to help you out, I hope you understand."

"I don't work for Farnsworth," I said, "I've never even met him."

"You're working for the same people who sent him up here, though. Roland's business associates, right? So why should I help you out?"

"Suppose we talk a deal," I said, "do a little trading, maybe."

"You gonna try to bribe me, Cruz? Farnsworth's people apparently didn't figure I was worth the trouble."

"Actually, I was thinking more along the lines of a friendly exchange of information."

"Yeah," he sighed, "I thought you might be. Pity. I could use the dough. Okay, so what have you got to trade?"

"The beach house," I said. "It's been burglarized and trashed. Kids, I'd guess. Probably a week or so ago."

"Damn," he said softly," we get a fair amount of that up here, but usually not till later in the year. Fair enough. What do you want to know?"

"For openers, the funeral. Why did Roland bury Charlie up here?"

"The Costas grew up in Algoma, Roland and Charlie. Their old man was a bootlegger back in the thirties, or so I'm told. After prohibition ended he moved on to bigger things in Detroit, but the family still has property here, the beach house, and the hunting lodge, a couple of odd lots. And they come up for a month or two every summer, and for the hunting season."

"You know them then? Personally, I mean?"

"Yeah," he said, taking a sip from his coffee, baring his teeth against the bite of it, "I've known 'em since they were kids, and everybody else in this town too. Hell, I even remember you when you played ball up at Laurance. You weren't half bad as I recall. And that's why I know those clowns aren't in Algoma, because if a chipmunk farts in the forest around here, I know about that too. Got anything else to trade?"

"Maybe. Look, you don't think the Costas are here, fine. The guy who hired me doesn't think so either. He only sent me up here because Farnsworth's people had problems with you and he wants to be sure they didn't overlook anything obvious. Dotting the *i*'s and crossing the *t*'s he called it."

"So?"

"So I don't like picking up after Farnsworth's army any more than you liked having 'em underfoot. So if you can think of anything they missed that might give me a line on where the Costas went, I'd greatly appreciate it."

"Yeah, I imagine you would. Only I'm not sure that helping you out is such a hot idea."

"You'd win my undying gratitude," I offered.

"Mmmm."

"Plus the satisfaction of making Farnsworth look like a schmuck."

"I could relate to that last part, at least," he said, sipping his coffee thoughtfully. "Is, ah, is that a Vietnam wire you're wearing?"

I fingered the slim gold strand around my right wrist. I've been wearing it so long I often forget I have it on. "That's right," I said, "so?"

"Nothing. My boy was there," he said, "two tours. '68 and '71. He didn't make it back from the second one. How about you?"

"A tour and a half, in '73. I made it back but not in one piece."

"A lot of folks didn't," he said quietly, "an awful lot of 'em."

I didn't say anything. He wasn't really talking to me.

"All right," he said abruptly, gulping the last of his coffee, "tell you what I'll do. I'm gonna do you one, Cruz, for Auld Lang Syne and because I really hate the idea of all those little *i*'s runnin' around without dots on 'em." He rose, winced as he slipped on his uniform jacket, and took an Algoma Wolves baseball cap with a badge pinned to it out of the top drawer of his desk. "Levina," he called, brushing his steel gray hair back and putting his cap on over it, "I'm gonna be gone maybe forty minutes, at the cemetery and the Windrift. You hold the fort, okay? Oh, and call Clint and tell him to check the Costa's beach house."

"The Windrift?" I said.

"That's right. They stayed there the day of the funeral."

"Not at the beach house?"

"Nope. It was already closed up for the season. Had it on

my extended surveillance list."

"Farnsworth's report didn't say anything about the Windrift."

"No kidding," he said blandly, "maybe I forgot to mention it to 'em. We had so many other things to talk about, ya see. You got your car here?"

"Out front."

"Good. No point in wastin' my county gas allotment on a wild goose chase. Let's go."

The woman behind the counter at the motel office was the one I'd seen coming out of bush-hat's cabin the night before. Up close, her resemblance to Rachel was less apparent. It was there, though, in the cheekbones and the auburn hair, but they were clearly a generation apart. The lady may have broken some hearts in her time, at barn dances or forest frolics, or whatever the locals did for jollies back then, but the years since hadn't been kind, and now the blush of surface capillaries in her cheeks matched the carelessly rinsed color of her hair.

"Mrs. Walker," LeClair nodded, "I'd like to look over your registry book please."

"We got a master criminal hidin' out here or something?" she asked, "and who's your friend?" Her diction had the forced precision of a serious drinker.

"He's one of your guests, Faye, and just let me see the book, okay?"

"Sure, sure," she shrugged, pushing the registry toward him. "Look, mister, if you have a complaint about your room—"

"It's nothing like that, Faye," LeClair sighed. "Roland Costa and Rol Junior stayed here the day of Charlie's funeral, right?"

"So? Is there some law against that now? They add a little class to this town if you ask me."

"I, ah, can't seem to find the entry for them here. When did they check in?"

"I'm not sure. They woke me up though, so it must've been early in the morning, seven or eight, I guess."

"Why isn't there an entry for them?"

"Hell, Ira, so there's no entry. So what? I'm not at the desk every minute. People pay in advance and they get a room and that's why we're in business, not to help you snoop—"

"What time did they leave?" LeClair interrupted.

"Leave? They, ah—" she coughed. "I'm not sure. The same day, I think. After the funeral."

"Well, was it afternoon, evening, or what?"

"I've already told you I'm not sure," she said sullenly, and for a moment her firm-jawed determination looked very familiar indeed. "Was there anything else, Ira?"

LeClair stared at her thoughtfully for a moment. She looked down at the countertop, carefully tracing the pattern in the Formica with her fingernail as though she'd never seen it before.

"No," LeClair said evenly, flipping the book closed. "I guess that'll be it, Faye. For now."

"Not exactly a fount of information," I said.

"She seemed a bit edgy," LeClair conceded, keeping his eyes on the road ahead as he skillfully piloted the Mustang between the potholes. We were headed northwest on a dirt road that had forked off the highway a mile or so north of the motel. Except for an occasional farmhouse, the countryside was as empty of people as the back of the moon.

"Faye's had a tough life," he continued, "she's got an invalid mother, and I doubt the motel does much more than break even. I, ah, had a little problem with her about a year ago, some money missing from a guest's room. I don't imagine I'm one of her favorite folks anymore. That's probably all it was."

"And her daughter?" I asked, casually, I hoped.

"Her daughter's a nice kid with troubles of her own, one of which is her mother," he said curtly, "why?"

"Your, ah, your deputy told me to stay away from her. For my own good, he said."

"Is that a fact?" LeClair said, glancing at me. "Well now, personally, if Clint offers me advice, I generally take it. Especially when he says it's for my own good."

"And if I decide not to take it?"

"Look, I offered to dot a couple of *i*'s for you, Cruz. I didn't say I'd write you a goddamn dictionary. You got problems with Clint over a girl, tell it to Ann Landers."

"Right," I said.

He slowed the car as we approached a line of weather-beaten, turn-of-the-century farmhouses huddled beside a white clapboard country church. A rust-bucket Chevy pickup truck was parked in the church's tiny gravel parking lot. LeClair pulled up beside it and we climbed out.

The church was in good condition for its age, but it had a forlorn, abandoned air about it, as though it was seldom used anymore. A cemetery covered most of the hill behind the church, an island mound in a sea of dry cornfields that stretched off almost to the horizon. A wrought iron sign above the entrance gate said Lovedale. The tombstones appeared to be a hodgepodge of eras, styles, and sizes, but the lanes were swept, the grass neatly trimmed, and not everyone in the cemetery was dead.

Two men were working on a plot halfway up the hillside, or rather one man was working, digging mechanically in a waist-deep grave, while the other was sitting with his back against a weathered headstone sipping a can of generic beer. The beer drinker was fortyish, barrel-shaped, wearing grubby bib overalls over a faded shirt of red-checked flannel. He was moonfaced, with grayish stubble and watery pouches beneath his eyes. Wispy spikes of dark brown hair shot with gray poked out from beneath his greasy engineer's cap. He lumbered unsteadily to his feet as we approached.

"Welcome to Lovedale, gents," he said, beaming with beery good-fellowship, "it ain't much as cemeteries go, but it's home. Hey Paulie, quit diggin' for a minute. We got comp'ny."

The digger was younger, but not much, mid-thirties maybe, lanky, with wide shoulders and an open, apple-pie face and sandy hair. A deep welt of a scar ran from his left temple, curving down to the nape of his neck. The hair bordering it was bone white. It must have been warm work, shoveling down in that hole, but his sweat-stained denim work shirt was buttoned at the cuffs and throat. He clambered eagerly up out of the grave with a grin like an April morning.

"Hey, Ira, good to see you."

"Good to see you too, Paulie," LeClair said. "Looks like Hec's got you doing most of the work, as usual."

"Ah, Paulie don't mind," the beer drinker said, "strong as an ox and twice as smart, right Paulie?"

"Sure Hec. You want me to keep shovelin'?"

"Take a break, Paulie," LeClair said, "I've got a few questions for you both." Hec's smile remained fixed, but I noticed a wariness in his eyes, and his grip tightened on the beer can.

"You want a beer, Ira?" he asked. "Paulie, run up to the toolshed and get Ira a cold one."

"I don't want a beer, Michaud, and the county doesn't pay Paulie to be your errand boy. This won't take long, so—"

"Jeezuz, no offense, Ira, but is this more crap about that funeral? We already told them guys from Detroit all we knew and then some. Who's your buddy here? He another one?"

"This is Mr. Cruz, Hec," LeClair said levelly, "and as far as you're concerned, we're working together temporarily. If that's okay with you."

"What kinda work you gonna have him doin', Ira," Hec sneered, "bean pickin' season's over."

LeClair shoved two stiff fingers into the beer drinker's chest, backing him up. Hec stumbled backward, lost his footing in the loose earth, and landed hard on his butt in the open grave without spilling his beer. He stared up at LeClair more in surprise than anger, and a momentary flicker of satisfaction showed in his eyes.

"You had no call to push me, Ira," he said slowly, "none at all."

"Maybe not," LeClair said, kneeling at the edge of the grave, "but there are a few things I've been meaning to discuss with you, Michaud, and today's as good a day as any. If I were you I'd just stay in that hole for a bit while we have our little talk. Paulie, you take Mr. Cruz up to the toolshed and get him a beer. He'll have some questions for you and you answer 'em. Okay?"

Paulie's eyes flicked uncertainly between the two men.

"Do what he says, Paulie," Hec said from the open grave, "maybe he'll wanna talk to Eugene too, while you're up there."

I was breathing hard when we reached the toolshed, but the climb didn't seem to affect Paulie at all. He took two cans of generic beer from a cheap foam cooler and handed me one.

"Cruz," he said, "that's a Mexican name, right?"

I nodded, and popped the cap on the beer.

"Was you in Vietnam?"

"That's right. How—?"

"I seen your bracelet. Couple guys I know got 'em. I been meaning to get one, but—hey, you know, I had a friend in 'Nam who was Mexican. I think he had a lotta names. You got a lotta names too?"

"Sure," I said, "Roberto Jose Andrew Mardo Flores Cruz." My saints' names rolled off my tongue with surprising ease. I hadn't spoken them in years.

"Flores," he echoed eagerly, "hey, that was my friend's name. It means 'flower', right?"

I nodded, and I couldn't help smiling. His grin was as contagious as a cough in a concert hall.

"Well, okay, Flower, why don't we pick out a comf'trble hunk o' dirt here and we can sit and drink our beers. Ira said you wanted to ask me about something?"

We both eased down to the grass, with our backs against the toolshed. We had an excellent view of the churchyard below, the roofs of the old houses along the road, and the fields of cornstalks that stretched along both sides of the highway. And we appeared to be quite alone.

"Maybe you should ask Eugene to come over," I said, glancing around uncertainly, "that way I won't have to ask the questions twice."

"You can ask him from here if you talk loud enough," Paulie said. "He's buried over there by the fence next to Major Gault."

I took a long, thoughtful pull from my beer before I glanced over at him. He was watching my reaction out of the corner of his eye, deadpan. "Gotcha," he said softly, the smile finally breaking through. "Don't worry, Flower, I ain't bananas. I still talk to Gene sometimes, but only to get a rise outa Hec. I know he's dead. Hell, I damn near died with him. We was best friends in high school, got drafted together, same outfit in Nam. We was even in the same foxhole when this dink grenade rolls in. We both tried to grab the damn thing to throw it out and wound up knockin' ourselves cockeyed instead. It woulda been pretty funny except then the grenade went off and Gene came here to Lovedale, and I wound up at the Vet's Facility in Grand Rapids for a couple years. Believe it or not, I like it better here in the cemetery."

"I can believe that," I said, "I did some time in a hospital myself. How long have you been working here?"

"I'm not really sure," he said, frowning, "Major Gault's been here since 1864 or maybe '62, and Gene's stone says 1973, but I'm not very good at numbers anymore, so I can't say exactly how long I been here. That's a funny thing about cemeteries. Once you're in one, time don't matter so much anymore. Like, the Major and Eugene lived maybe a hundred years apart, but now they're here together, maybe swapping war stories and stuff. At least I hope so." He lapsed into a thoughtful silence, sipping his beer.

"A month or so ago there was a funeral here," I said, "Charles Costa's. Do you remember that?"

"Sure I remember it. I ain't simple, you know. It's just numbers I have trouble with, things like that."

"Sorry," I said, "I didn't mean—well, anyway, were both you and Hec working that day?"

"Nah, just me. The funeral was on a Saturday and Hec don't like to work Saturdays. It was a funny one, though."

"How do you mean, funny?"

"It was prob'ly the biggest sendoff I ever seen, and I've seen a few, you know? See that big ugly hunk o' marble with the cedars planted around it? Like they were keepin' it away from the riffraff in the rest of the cemetery? That's Costa's. Sucker's really somethin', isn't it? And you shoulda seen his casket. I guess his box musta been standard size 'cause it fit in the frame, but it sure looked bigger, real shiny copper with burled walnut inserts. Probably cost more'n Hec and me make in a year. Weighed a ton, too. Maybe that was the problem."

"Problem?"

"Ahh, after the funeral, the director couldn't get the gearbox that lowers the casket to work. I had to unjam it for 'im. But that ain't what I meant about it bein' funny. See, the funeral director wasn't a local guy. He was from Detroit, Claudio somethin' or other, and he musta had at least a dozen assistants with him, all dressed up like headwaiters and scramblin' around here puttin' out flowers and stuff like it's a school gym on prom night, and Claudio's havin' a heart attack 'cause the monument stone hadn't been delivered yet. And then, after they got the place all decked out like a Polack wedding, nobody came. Nobody. Just Rol Costa Junior and his old man. Just the two of 'em."

"They were here, then? You saw them?"

"Oh yeah. I know Rol from hangin' around at the beach and stuff, you know. Him and his dad showed up in this big silver Lincoln, stuck ol' Charlie in the ground, and that was that."

"And no one else was around other than the funeral people, you, and Hec?"

"I just said that," he said with a trace of annoyance, "nobody. And Hec wasn't here either. He don't like workin' Saturdays."

"It looks like you do most of the work even when he is here."

"Could be," he shrugged, "it don't matter. Look, I know

Hec maybe takes advantage of me a little, but I don't care. I'm just glad to be outa that hospital and doin' *somethin'*, even if it's only diggin' graves. I mean, somebody's gotta do it, right? Besides, Hec stands up for me sometimes, like with old lady Stansfield. She's got that house near the west fence, and she don't like me, you know? So when we got this complaint about me workin' out here with no shirt on, I figured who it was and I asked Hec to talk to her about it and he did. He don't get many complaints about my work, though. This place looks pretty nice, don't it, Flower? Maybe not to move into, but you know what I mean."

"It looks very nice, Paulie," I agreed, "anybody can see you put a lot of care into it. When did the Costas leave?"

"After the funeral, I guess," he said, frowning. "I ain't really sure though. I was pooped out so I grabbed some *z*'s behind the toolshed here."

"Thanks," I said, "I appreciate your help." Without thinking, I slipped the thin gold band from around my wrist and handed it to him.

"Hey, Flower," he said, his eyes widening, "you don't have to give me nothing. I mean, I'm just glad to have somebody to talk to, you know?"

"It's all right," I said. "I, ah, I've got another one at home, Paulie. Take this one. Please."

"You sure it's okay?" he said doubtfully, "I mean, I been wantin' to get me one, but, well anyway, thanks a lot." He slid it carefully on his wrist, admiring it as it caught the glint of the mid-morning sun. "Gee, I wish I had something I could—" He fumbled in the breast pocket of his faded denim workshirt. "Hey, you want a couple joints? Here."

"No thanks," I said, "I—"

"Go ahead," he said, "it's not bad stuff."

"Okay," I said, accepting one of the smoothly rolled cigarettes. "But just one, all right. I don't want to do you out of your stash."

"Nah, don't worry about that. I got some more at my place."

"Really? No trouble connecting up here?"

"You ever do a long boonie recon in 'Nam?" he asked, smiling slyly.

"A few," I nodded.

"Same kinda thing," he said. "I get my stuff by livin' off the bounty of the land."

I glanced around and for a moment the cemetery and the fields around it had the scent of danger. Like the jungle. But only for a moment. "I think I'd better be going," I said, getting to my feet. "I see the sheriff's helping Hec out of his hole."

We drove most of the way back to Algoma in silence, each of us lost in his own thoughts. "Paulie told me they were here, and then they left," I said at last, "you get anything useful from Hec?"

"Nope," LeClair said, "and I don't think he's gonna vote for me in the next election either. He told me he wasn't there the day of the funeral."

"Paulie said the same thing."

"Well then, I guess that about covers it. I can't think of anyone else they would have seen when they were here. They're not a particularly sociable bunch, the Costas."

"No," I said, "I don't imagine they are. Look, I, ah, appreciate your help on this thing."

"No charge," he sighed, "it comes with the territory. Tell you something though, if I were you, I'd just kick back and enjoy a little vacation on the expense account. Do a little fishing maybe. The Costas are a hard lot, all of 'em, and they've spent a lotta time around here. They know the land, the people. And from what the state boys tell me they're nobody to mess with even in Motown. There's no way they'd hang around up here for long. They'd stand out like a hooker at a church picnic."

"Have you ever had trouble with them?"

"Some," he conceded. "Rol Junior got into a scuffle a couple years back with a local punk down at the lake. Roughed him up pretty good, and the kid's family talked lawsuit for about fifteen minutes."

"Why'd they drop it? Threats?"

"Nope, just the opposite. For openers, they didn't have a legal leg to stand on, it was just a push-and-shove that got outa hand, and nobody was sure who started it. Rol Junior sure as hell finished it in a hurry, though. He's one mean little bastard, Junior. Then Roland took mom and pop aside for a friendly chat and that was that. I think they got a new car out of it. Anyway, they dropped the charges, which was all I cared about."

"Do you remember the other kid's name?"

"Sure. Slominski. Danny, I think. But he doesn't live up here anymore."

"No? Why not?"

"What do you mean, why not? When you got out of high school did you stick around?"

"No," I said, "I left, but—"

"Right. You got out. And so did I, once. And so do most kids from up here. Hell, unemployment runs thirty-five percent in this county year 'round. The scenery's nice, but you can't eat it, and most people up here barely scrape by."

"It can't be all bad," I said. "You came back."

"I had no choice," he said, swerving the Ford sharply to avoid a pothole, "my dad got sick and couldn't do for himself.

But most folks head for parts south, so don't read anything heavy into Danny Slominski not bein' around anymore. Two thirds of the local kids get out. Like you did."

I let it pass. I had a hunch it wasn't Danny Slominski's leaving that bothered him. It was another kid who'd left. And hadn't made it back. "Paulie mentioned a funeral director named Claudio," I said, changing the subject. "Does the name ring a bell?"

"Rigoni's Funeral Home. They handled all the arrangements but they're not from around here. From Detroit, I think. Legitimate, as far as I know, but I had no reason to check 'em out."

"Maybe I'll look them up when I get home, but it doesn't sound like much."

LeClair pulled the Mustang over to the curb in front of the Sheriff's Department. "Home sweet office," he sighed. "Well. Sorry you didn't dig up any major clues, but I told you so. You heading back to Detroit?"

"Maybe I'll take your advice and take a mini-vacation on the expense account. Do a little sightseeing. I don't get out of the city much, and you've got a nice little town here."

"We like it. If you need anything else, just ask. You may not get it, but you can ask. Somebody usually knows where to find me. I'll see you around, Cruz." He flipped me a mock salute and strode off toward his office.

I sat there a moment, watching him go, mulling over bits and pieces of the morning; Paulie's easy grin, Hec sitting down hard in the open grave, Rachel's anguish over the rabbit. And the crunch of small bones. Damn.

I slid over behind the wheel, swung the Ford into a U-turn and headed back to the motel to change clothes. At least part of what I'd told LeClair was true. I was definitely going to do some more sightseeing.

Chapter

Nine

The Windrift's parking lot was nearly a third full, but I would have noticed the car in the middle of a Motown rush hour. A midnight blue State Police cruiser was parked in front of the motel office. Interesting. Even more interesting was the fact that Faye Walker was standing in front of my cabin, her arms folded, foot tapping impatiently. And the door to my room was open.

I parked the Mustang a few cabins down and climbed out. Faye shot me a look of pure venom, then turned and stalked off toward the motel office without a word. Curiouser and curiouser.

I approached the open door cautiously and peered around the jamb. There were two State troopers, both in uniform. The taller one was dark-haired, square-shouldered and square faced with only a rudimentary neck in between. He was standing in front of the closet riffling through my clothes. The other cop was squat and beefy with a chubby, florid face and pale blond hair and eyebrows. He wouldn't have looked out of place plodding barefoot through the dirt behind a mule and harrow, and he looked just as at home lounging in the easy chair beside my bed, his hands folded placidly in his lap. I stepped into the doorway.

"You gentlemen have five seconds to explain what you're

doing here," I said, "and then I'm going to call a cop."

"Your landlady gave us permission to wait for you here, Mr. Cruz," the pudgy one said calmly, "we didn't figure you'd mind."

"Was your buddy going to wait in the closet?" I said.

"It was open," No-neck said, "I was just admiring your taste in clothes. You haven't got any. I thought mobsters were all supposed to be snappy dressers, you know, black silk shirts, white ties, and like that."

"That's odd, I thought I closed it before I left," I said. "Must've forgotten. Why don't you close it for me now. Unless you can show me a warrant. Now what's this all about?"

"Routine police business," the pudgy one said, "are you Roberto Andrew Cruz?"

"That's right."

"Could I see some identification please?"

"Sure," I said, "if you don't mind showing me yours." I opened my wallet and handed him my driver's license, and he took a picture ID tag out of his breast pocket. It was a bad likeness, but it was close enough: Lieutenant Francis X. Schmitke.

"I'm Lieutenant Schmitke," he said formally, "and this is Corporal Yaeger. I believe you have a permit to carry a concealed weapon, Mr. Cruz. Are you carrying one now?"

"Nope," I said, and opened my coat to prove it. I didn't have to, maybe Mike Hammer wouldn't have, but I try not to rile cops unnecessarily. They're a nervous lot, and rightly so. And they carry guns, and handcuffs, and they can cause you all sorts of problems if they choose to, with or without cause. So I don't knuckle my forehead, or call them 'sir', but I open my coat once in awhile.

"Thank you," Schmitke nodded, "I hate talking with people wearing guns."

93

"I'm not sure how much talking we're going to do anyway," I said, "unless you boys are the Welcome Wagon."

"Oh, we're not here to hassle you, Mr. Cruz," Schmitke said, "this is just a courtesy call. You know, when a cop visits a strange town, he'll usually stop by the local precinct house or sheriff's office or whatever, just to say hello. You're not a cop anymore, but you're still in the same business, in a way, so we thought we'd save you a trip."

"What business are you talking about? Collecting back child support? Dead skips on car payments? That's mostly what I do now."

"Lost and found, Mr. Cruz, lost and found. The problem is, we're all looking for the same person, though for slightly different reasons."

"The same person?" I said.

"Let's not get into the old soft shoe here, Cruz," Schmitke said mildly, "I'm talking about Cindy Stanek, Charlie Costa's girlfriend. Since you've got no record for wet work, I presume that's Lugo's end of it, but either way, I want you to know it's not gonna happen on my turf. We're not out of touch just because we're up here in the woods. This is the age of the computer, LEIN, the law enforcement information net. You're a new entry in our computer, Cruz, under 'associates with known organized crime connections.' First B.C. and O. And now Enrique Lugo. You're moving in pretty fast company."

"I'm not looking for Cindy Stanek," I said, "and I don't know anybody named Lugo."

"He's gonna play it dumb," Yaeger said, "you're bein' too polite, Frank. You're always too polite."

"Computers don't lie, Cruz," Schmitke said patiently, "only people. But maybe I can jog your memory a little. Enrique Lugo? From Tucson? Did nine years in the state pen at Florence for second-degree homicide. Arrested in connection with violent crimes in the Detroit area four times in the past six years, and once down in Akron. No convictions. Witnesses in two of those cases were murdered. Shotgunned. At present Lugo's carried on the books as head of Bradleigh, Childreth and Osbourne's maintenance section, but his real job is what it's always been. He kills people. For Eladio Delagarza. He's very good at it. And he's registered at this motel, four cabins down from yours. Sound familiar to you yet, Mr. Cruz?"

"Jesus H. Christ," I said softly.

"So don't bother waltzing us around, Cruz. We know who you are and why you're here, and it's not gonna happen. So why don't you pack up your bags and haul your ass out of my district. And take your gorilla with you."

"Get outa Dodge by sundown? Something like that?"

"Sundown's at least five hours away. Why wait?"

"I'm afraid it's not that simple. I'm not going anywhere, or at least, not today."

"I don't think you heard the Lieutenant," Yaeger said, "he told—"

"Corporal," I said, cutting him off, "there was a time when I took a lot of orders from a lot of lieutenants, but that was a long time ago. Have you been on the force long, Schmitke?"

"Almost twenty. Why?"

"And you're a lieutenant, so I assume you're moderately bright."

"Moderately. What's your point?"

"Just this, and you can take notes if you like. One, I am not looking for Cindy Stanek. Two, until a moment ago, I never heard of whatsisname Lugo."

"Enrique."

"Fine, Enrique. Now it seems to me this can go two ways. You can hassle me, and I call Bradleigh to see how fast he can file a harassment suit, and we all look like Shemp, Larry and Moe. Or we can reason together, to see if we can salvage anything out of the situation."

"You gotta be kidding," Yaeger said.

"Shut up, Harry," Schmitke said quietly. "Is there a bottom line to this, Cruz?"

"Yup, but you're not going to like it much. You're the second cop who assumed I was looking for the girl. I'm not, but the people who sent me up here could have sent me after her, or at least told me to keep an eye out for her. Only they didn't. It never even came up. I think they already know where she is."

"You're right," Schmitke nodded, "I don't like it much. Okay, just for the sake of argument, let's say you're not looking for the girl. What are you doing here?"

"Sorry," I said, "we can discuss what I'm *not* doing here, the rest comes under the heading of confidential."

"Except that we already know you're working for the Delagarza people," Schmitke said reasonably, "so why bother to protect them? I can flat guarantee they wouldn't do the same for you."

"Maybe not, but it doesn't have anything to do with them. Or you. Only me. Sorry."

"You think the girl's dead, don't you." It wasn't a question.

"What do you think?"

"I'm afraid she probably is," he sighed. "I thought so when Farnsworth's army was blundering around up here. They asked a lot of people a lot of questions, but not about her. Still, until otherwise notified, department policy is that she's still alive and we'll keep looking for her. Too bad.

Judging from her pictures she was a fox. So what about Lugo? You claim he's not with you, then what's he doing here?"

"I really don't know. Maybe I'll look into it."

"Yeah," Schmitke said, getting to his feet, "I would if I were you. But if you're going to be hanging around, and I hear that either one of you ask any questions about the girl, we'll be back. And we'll be unhappy. Come on, Harry."

The corporal brushed past me on his way out the door. None too gently.

"Hey, Lieutenant," I said, and he paused in the doorway. "Did you know that the coffin jammed?"

"What are you talking about?"

"Charlie Costa's coffin. When they tried to lower it into the grave, the mechanism jammed. The guy at the cemetery said he thought it was too heavy."

"So?" he said, puzzled.

"So, I was told that maybe Roland Costa aced Charlie himself. Do you think he'd have done that if the girl was free, knowing she'd panic and run right back to the police for protection as soon as she heard about it?"

"What are you suggesting, that he killed them both at the same time? And maybe got rid of them at the same place?"

"All I'm saying is, the coffin jammed. Maybe because it was too heavy. That's all. But it's something to think about, isn't it."

"Yeah," he said, "maybe it is. Are you sure about this, about it jamming, I mean?"

"That's what the man said."

"So why tell me about it? Assuming you're not just jerking me around, seems to me you could have problems with your boss if he found out."

"Just being a good citizen," I said. "Look, I hired on to do a job, and so I'll try to do it. But I don't have to like it."

"I guess you don't," he said. "Life's a bitch, ain't it?"

"Right," I agreed, "and then you die. Are you going to do anything about that coffin?"

"Uh huh." he nodded, "I'm gonna think about it. We'll see you around, Cruz. Count on it."

Chapter

Ten

I stood in the doorway of my motel room and watched them walk to their cruiser. Yaeger climbed in behind the wheel. Schmitke got in the passenger's side, slouched with his hat tipped down over his eyes, and assumed the guise of a load of grubby clothing on its way to the laundromat.

They sat out there talking for a few minutes, and I was beginning to think they were staking me out, when Yaeger gunned the cruiser back, did a half-spin, and roared out of the parking lot in a cloud of dust.

I strolled out to my car, noting room four-twenty-two as I passed. It looked exactly like the others. Except for the gleaming new Saxony red Caddy Seville convertible parked in front of it. I should have guessed. Maybe crime doesn't pay, but some of the perks aren't bad. Not bad at all.

I caressed the Caddy's hood again on the way back. Someday. Maybe sooner than I'd expected the way things were going. I wondered if I could buy a black silk shirt and white necktie at the Algoma five-and-dime.

I opened the Mustang's trunk, retrieved my nearly empty suitcase, and carried it back to my room.

I shucked my blue impress-your-local-cop suit and changed into blue jeans, a light blue L.L. Bean chamois shirt, and Hi Land walking boots. Then I popped the suitcase open, took out my nine-millimeter Beretta 92 automatic, and checked the action. There are better handguns than the Beretta on the market now, the Smith and Wesson Model 59, and Heckler and Koch makes a piece that holds fifteen rounds and only has four moving parts, but I've owned the Model 92 for a few years, I can demolish a paper plate with it at forty yards, and when I strap it on I don't tilt anymore.

I slipped the Bianchi shoulder rig on, slid one loaded clip into the spare ammo pouch, the other into the Model 92, jacked a round into the chamber, set the safety, and shoved the gun into the wet-molded leather holster under my left arm.

I put my navy blue windbreaker on, kicked my suitcase under the bed, and locked the door to my room behind me when I left. Not that it would make much difference, apparently, if you knew the manager. I walked down to room four-twenty-two and rapped on the door. There was no answer. I raised my hand to rap again when the door opened quickly, about four inches. I caught a glimpse of dark eyes but not much else, then he closed the door, unhooked the chain bolt, and opened it again. "Come on in."

He stalked back to the bed and flopped down on it, with his back against the headboard. The wreckage of a *USA Today* was strewn around the bed. He picked up the sports page and began scanning it, frowning.

"Mi casa es su casa," he said, "there's beer in the cooler by the door there if you want one."

He was smaller than I'd expected, five seven or eight, but solidly built, with a muscular frame that looked hard as a crowbar. He appeared to be in his mid-forties, his dark hair was thinning a bit at the back, with a sprinkling of silver at the temples, his face was bronzed and angular. His cheeks were pocked with acne craters, but they only lent character to an otherwise unremarkable face. He was wearing a canary yellow cashmere sweater over a medium blue oxford cloth shirt, button-down collar, navy dress slacks, and black socks. A pair of Gucci tasseled loafers peered up at me from under the edge of the bed.

"You're Lugo?" I said.

"That's right," he said quietly, glancing up at me for a moment. His eyes were dark and feral and intelligent, a carnivore's eyes, black as anthracite. "There's a letter for you in the briefcase on the chair there."

I walked over and picked up the briefcase. It was tan, glove leather, kangaroo, I think, with bound brass corners, and it probably cost as much as my car. I opened it. One envelope. With my name on it.

The letter was on Bradleigh, Childreth and Osbourne stationery.

Mr. Roberto A. Cruz,

This is to introduce to you Mr. Enrique Lugo, an employee of B.C.&O., who is to be considered by you as our designated representative in the matter for which you were engaged. Please inform Mr. Lugo of all relevant developments as they occur, and accept whatever instructions or directions Mr. Lugo may deem appropriate as though—blah, blah, blah.

There was more legal boilerplate, but the gist of it was in the first paragraph. Apparently I had a new boss. Terrific.

"Any questions?" he asked, without looking up.

"One or two," I said, "you've been here since yesterday. Why didn't you show me this before?"

"You're the detective," he said, "I figured you were any

good, you'd find me. Took you long enough. Those cops tell you I was here?"

I nodded.

"Kinda stand out up here, don't we? Two *hombres* in paddyland. They probably ain't seen this many brown faces since they killed off the *Indios*."

"Lugo," I sighed, "I'm afraid we have a problem."

"No," he said positively, "we got no problem. The letter tells you what you need to know, right?"

"It's not quite that simple. I hired on to look for the Costas. I didn't hire on to set them up for a hit."

"Cops," he smiled, shaking his head, "is that what they tol' you? That I'm some kinda button man?"

"That's right."

"What if I told you different," he said, meeting my gaze, "who would you believe?"

"Them, probably."

He stared at me a moment, then resumed reading his paper. "It don't matter what you think," he said, "but just for the record, I ain't here to hurt anybody. I'm just a businessman on vacation. Besides, if I was here to pop them Costas, I wouldn't be out in the open at this motel, and I wouldn't be alone, neither. They're pretty good, those two. Especially together. I'm better, but I still wouldn't try to take 'em down by myself. Unless for *honor* or something. The letter—"

I wadded the letter into a ball and bounced it gently off his chest. He glanced up from his paper, startled.

"What the fuck was that for?"

"Tell Bradleigh I'll return his fee, minus time and expenses. Have a nice day."

"Where do you think you're going?"

"Back to Detroit," I said, "I'm out."

"Whaddya mean you're out? You're not out unless— Hey! wait a minute!"

I paused with my hand on the doorknob.

"Look, you don't just walk away, *hombre*. Not from me."

"Why not? Why should I worry about a vacationing businessman?"

He took a deep breath, and let it out slowly in a silent whistle. "Look, this is stupid," he said at last, "you walk out now, we both look like *payasos*. Just cool it, okay? Now what's your problem?"

"You. You weren't part of the deal. I don't do wet work."

"Look, I told you I ain't here to hit anybody, and I'm not."

"Then why are you here?"

"The same damn reason you are. For a vacation. Look, Cruz, Roland had some trouble with his brother, but he took care of it, he did what he had to do. Only maybe he's not sure what he did was enough, you dig? So he decides to lay low till things cool off. I don't blame him, either. The old man has his moods and when he's in one, gone is the best place to be. But Roland wouldn't hide out up here. It's the first place we'd look if we wanted to punch his ticket. He's probably down in Bimini or the Caymans maybe, soakin' up the sun, while we're up here freezin' our *cojones*, just so Bradleigh can tell the old man we looked every-fuckin'-where for 'em. Nobody's mad at nobody. The old man just wants to put this thing in the past and get on with business. You turn up Roland or Rollie, you tell 'em that. Tell 'em I'll meet 'em anyplace they say to talk. Only you ain't gonna 'cause they ain't up here. If you get lucky and fall over somethin' to give us a line on where they went, just let me know about it, I'll tell Bradleigh to give you a bonus, and we can both get the fuck outa this dump. See? No problem."

"That's all I have to do if I find them? Pass a message?"

"That's it. And you prob'ly won't hafta do that much."

"And what are you going to be doing while I look?"

"Whaddya mean? What I do is none of your fuckin' business."

"Sure it is. I don't want you looking over my shoulder, Lugo. If I see you there, for any reason at all, I'm out."

"You worry too much, Cruz. Christ, I ain't goin' around chasin' after you. I'm on vacation. You do what you want, just let me know how it's goin'. Think you can handle that?"

"I suppose so," I said. "Where will you be?"

"Here, mostly. Maybe I'll drive over to Laurance later, buy a VCR. I can't believe a fuckin' town with no cable TV."

"It's a poor area up here. Not many people."

"We was poor back in Tucson too, but at least we had TV. Somebody's TV," he added dryly. "Anything else on your mind?"

"The Costas' beach house has been burglarized. Whoever did it trashed the place pretty good."

"You think it's got anything to do with them takin' off?"

"I don't think so. Kids, most likely."

"Prob'ly," he agreed, picking up his paper again, "little bastards today are all nuts. Don't steal stuff, just wreck it. All nuts. You see Roland, don't tell him about the house. It'll piss him off and he's risky business when he's pissed off. Ask Charlie. You wanna hand me one of them beers?"

"No," I said, "I wouldn't."

He looked up at me, his face expressionless, with absolutely nothing showing in his eyes that I could read. "Good," he said at last, "I wasn't thirsty anyway. You know, you oughta loosen up a little, Roberto. You and me might just get along."

"I doubt that," I said.

"Yeah," he nodded, "so do I. Stay in touch. And don't let the door hit you in the ass on your way out."

Chapter

Eleven

I stopped at my cabin long enough to grab the blaze-orange vest. I didn't drop off the gun. I was getting a very bad feeling about the way things were shaping up. Climbing into the Mustang, I fired it up, considered driving into Algoma to grab a hot sand. for breakfast, then decided the hell with it. I checked my map, then gunned the Mustang out of the parking lot and headed north, toward the Costas' hunting lodge in the Ojibwa foothills.

As I drove past the turnoff to the cemetery, I could see a dozen or so cars parked in the churchyard. A green canopy had been set up on the hill over the grave Paulie'd been digging earlier and the ceremony was underway. It was too far to make out any faces, but I thought I could see Paulie sitting alone up by the toolshed. And I wondered if he was watching the proceedings. Or talking to a friend.

Either way, it was a great day for a funeral, or almost anything else. The air was cool and crisp under a pastel blue November sky. It didn't look like it would last long, though. A heavy cloudbank was drifting slowly up from the southwest, tall and dark as a mountain, towering above the desiccated cornstalks rippling beneath it in the distance.

Eight or nine miles out I turned off onto the gravel road that led into the foothills. The Ojibwa Mountains loomed ahead, narrow, craggy ridges that really aren't much taller than the hills that surround them, nowhere near as tall as the Porcupine Mountains in the upper peninsula, and in Arizona, where Lugo came from, they probably wouldn't be considered mountains at all.

Still, they have a beauty of their own, especially the foothills, rolling, forested mounds that stretch off to the horizon like timber-covered waves, colored by aspen and birch still wearing some of their leaves in the lowlands, gradually darkening to thick forests of pine near the crests.

According to my map, the Costas' hunting lodge was only twelve miles northwest of Algoma as the crow flies, but I wasn't flying a crow. I was piloting a rented Ford Mustang that wasn't designed for the rutted gravel roads that coiled and twisted up into the foothills. The car yawed and pitched like a raft in a typhoon, bottoming out on its rear axle and occasionally scraping gravel with a fender. I slowed it to a crawl to avoid kissing my damage deposit goodbye.

The hill country wasn't virgin forest, of course, but it wasn't far from it. There was almost no sign of human life up here, no power or telephone lines, no mailboxes, only the crude gravel road, and now and again a private drive, usually with the name of a hunting club beside it; Brigadoon, Big Bear, the Marilyn X. I was still wondering what the X stood for when I passed one that read Costa on a wide, chain link gate set well off the road.

I slowed the Mustang to a halt, shifted into reverse, and backed up down the middle of the road, which is not something I'd do ordinarily, but I hadn't seen another car since I'd turned into the hills.

I pulled into the driveway facing the gate, but I didn't turn the car off. I climbed out and walked to the gate instead, and tried a couple of the keys from the ring I'd lifted from the beach house on the padlock. And got lucky. The third key opened it.

I looked over the lay of the land. There was no sign of a house or anything else, so I swung the gate open, the shriek of rusty hinges ringing loud in the rustling silence.

I drove the Ford about forty yards, then pulled it off the driveway behind a copse of cedars, out of sight of the road. No point in arousing the curiosity of anyone who happened by. Neighbors tend to look out for each other up here, and this time of the year most of them would be carrying guns. A reassuring thought. I jogged back to the gate, swung it closed, and relocked it. Then I set off down the driveway.

Moving as quietly as possible, I avoided fallen branches and dry leaves, but made no attempt to avoid being seen. I was wearing the blaze-orange vest and kept to the center of the drive. The only thing missing was a bull's-eye painted on my chest. Still, if the Costas were as good as everybody seemed to think, it was unlikely I could take them by surprise, and they might be strung tight enough to drop anybody they spotted sneaking around on sight. I just hoped they wouldn't blow away a klutz who sashayed up their driveway in broad daylight wearing a stupid orange vest.

The woods seemed especially silent after the engine hum and gravel crunching of the car. No insects were buzzing, they were dead or aestivating, the songbirds had already migrated south. There was only the creaking and sighing of the trees as the wind moved through the upper branches, and the occasional distant boom of a hunting rifle, rolling and echoing through the hills like thunder.

Usually it was a lone shot. A spooked or wounded buck usually moves too quickly in heavy cover to allow a second shot. You either take him with number one, or he's gone. But a few times I heard the *pop-pop-pop* of a semi-automatic rifle.

In the forest, as in the army, firepower is gradually supplanting marksmanship. The theory is that if you throw enough lead, you'll eventually get lucky and hit something—only in Vietnam we found out the hard way that it just ain't so. The flaw is that the theory requires some luck on the part of the shooter, and anyone in the middle of a war obviously doesn't have any to spare.

I might have taken some comfort in the general decline of marksmanship in the modern world if I hadn't seen those pictures of Roland Junior gloating over the dead bucks. Some people can still shoot, apparently. And if the stories were true, Roland Senior had popped his own brother twice behind the ear. A feat like that requires more than just marksmanship. A lot more.

I'd trudged a good three-quarters of a mile and was beginning to wonder if I'd missed it somehow, when I rounded a curve in the drive and found the hunting lodge. It was smaller than the beach house, but similar, pre-fabricated and trucked into the site. It was finished with bright yellow aluminum siding, sitting on a raw-looking concrete foundation on a wooded bluff that overlooked a broad, grassy meadow.

The view was attractive enough, the meadow was seventy or eighty yards across with a stream running through the middle of it, and the woods beyond looked dark and inviting. A log cabin or a naturally finished clapboard sided home would have blended in, but the garish yellow pre-fab was as out of place as a tattoo on a plaster saint.

I approached the lodge cautiously, keeping my hands in plain sight. "Hello? Anybody home?"

My voice seemed surprisingly loud, but I didn't startle anyone in the cabin, apparently. They didn't reply. Or blow me out of my socks.

I moved warily up to the front door and knocked. "Hello?"

No answer. I opened the screen door, but didn't bother to knock again. A glass panel had been punched out of the inner door. And the door was unlocked.

I reached inside my jacket and jerked the Beretta out of its holster, eased the safety off, then nudged the front door gently open with my foot. There was no sound in the cabin, not even the ticking of a clock. Nothing. There's a ninjitsu training method in which a blindfolded student is sent through a series of rooms to teach him to sense human proximity. If he misses anybody, he gets whacked with a wooden sword as he passes. I've never had that training, but I had a visceral sense that the lodge was as empty as the beach house had been. And it was in the same condition. I stepped inside.

The layout was straightforward, a combined kitchen and living room with sliding glass doors that opened onto a deck overlooking the meadow, two bedrooms and a bath in the rear. The place had been torn apart, sofas and chairs slashed and overturned, lamps smashed, pictures smashed, magazines ripped to pieces and tossed around. Home sweet home.

I checked both bedrooms and the bath quickly. They'd been trashed as well, but somehow the sense of violation seemed less intense. The rooms contained nothing personal, no photographs, or clothing. Or S&M magazines. They were as anonymous as metropolitan motel units. The bath reeked of English Leather. A bottle of aftershave had been smashed in the sunshine yellow tub. The medicine cabinet mirror had been shattered and the shower doors kicked in. The cloying scent reminded me of something though, and I walked back to the living room.

There was no stench. The refrigerator door was open and the contents were strewn around, but there was no mold, and no odor. I knelt near the mess and examined it. Dented cans of soup, sugar, dry cereal. It was a mess but it hadn't rotted.

There was nothing perishable in it. No milk or cheese or juice. Which indicated that no one had used the cabin in some time. If the Costas were hiding out, they hadn't been doing it here.

The theory of kids trashing the place was gone too. One house maybe, but two, twenty miles apart? No chance. Still, there was that size seven footprint. And the dime-store safe that the burglars couldn't open. Maybe not kids, but not pros either.

I moved warily through the jumble in the living room, nudging things around with my foot. There was something vaguely wrong about the room, something missing. It just didn't feel like a hunting lodge. There were a few trophies mixed in the shambles, a mounted rainbow trout, a couple of stuffed ducks, even an eight-point rack of antlers, but . . .

There were no gun racks in the mess. And no marks where any had been torn from the walls, either. There wasn't a single place in the room to hang a rifle. Odd.

I circled the room, tapping on the walls as I moved, and found what I was looking for next to the bar. A large, hinged panel, its seams cleverly aligned with the rest of the wall to make it nearly invisible. I swung it open to reveal a taupe-colored texture-painted steel door, roughly five feet tall and forty inches wide. A Treadlok gun safe. And this one was no dime-store cheapo. It was roughly a thousand dollars worth of quarter inch steel plate bolted into the wall. The vandals had apparently missed it, but it wouldn't have made any difference if they'd found it. If they couldn't open the other safe, they couldn't even make this one mad. And neither could I, unless . . .

I riffled through the key ring I'd lifted from the beach house and found the brass plate with the engraved series of numbers. I tried them on the combination lock, and *voila*, the counterbalanced steel door swung open, smooth and well-oiled as an evangelist's handshake.

The safe contained more than a dozen-odd weapons, and odd was the word for some of them. There were four handguns in a rack mounted on the door, two Llama Omni double-action automatics in nine-millimeter, an Ingram Mac 10 machine pistol in the same caliber, and an Iver Johnson 'Enforcer,' which is a shortened version of the M-1 carbine. The Enforcer was loaded with two fifty-round banana clips taped together jungle-style. Not exactly your ordinary pop-and-the-kids beer can buster. I checked the other three pistols as well. Also loaded.

The shotguns were really too pretty to shoot, three matched sets of Beretta skeet and trap guns, beautifully engraved with woodland scenes, inlaid with gold. I didn't recognize the artisan's name, but that didn't mean anything. I don't know who draws "Andy Capp" either, but I know quality work when I see it.

Three of the rifles were engraved too, a Colt Sauer Grand African .458 Magnum, and a pair of Sako Safari grades, handy to have around if a bull elephant starts rooting up your rutabagas, but a bit too much gun for anything on this continent.

The other rifles were all paramilitary types, Uzi submachine guns, Colt AR-15s, a pair of Ruger Mini-14s in stainless steel with extended magazines, fifty rounds each. Not hunting guns by any stretch of the imagination. Unless you were hunting people. There was enough nine-millimeter and .223 ammunition in the bottom of the safe to start world war III, and several boxes each for the big game rifles and shotguns. A half dozen slots in the safe were unused, but I had no way of telling whether guns were missing or not.

I did some quick mental arithmetic, adding up the value of

the weapons in the safe, and came up with a figure somewhere between forty and fifty thousand dollars. Which meant
I was wrong about the three hundred bucks in the beach
house safe. It wasn't small change for these characters, it was
barely bus fare. I reluctantly swung the safe door closed. I
didn't know whether it contained the price of my integrity or
not, but it might. I decided to think about that later.

What concerned me at the moment was who had trashed
these places and why. The footprint at the beach house was a
kid's or possibly a woman's. But it only proved that one
person with a relatively small foot had been there, not necessarily that they'd been there alone. Were they looking for
something? Possibly, but the mess seemed too extreme to be
the result of a search or even a cover for one. Besides, the furniture and bedding hadn't really been pawed through thoroughly, only slashed, and you can't hide much in a bottle of
aftershave. Plus, whoever it was had given up on the safe.

I stood there, hands on my hips, looking the room over.
Anger, I thought. I could almost feel it radiating from the debris like warmth from a fresh wound. But who was angry
about what? Damned if I knew. Sherlock Holmes could probably deduce the guy's social security number from the way
the mold was climbing the beach house cupboards. All I was
sure of was that one of the people involved was fairly small,
and that somebody was probably mad at somebody. Elemen-
tary, my dear Cruz.

Enough. The sunlight was beaming through the sliding
glass patio doors and I suddenly felt the need to be out of that
room and into the fresh air. I unlatched the door, slid it open,
and stepped out onto the deck that overlooked the meadow.
Maybe the Costas had lame taste in vacation homes, but they
certainly knew where to build them. The meadow stretched
away for roughly eighty yards. It appeared to be natural, there

were no stumps sticking up anywhere, and I guessed that the soil around the stream was too sandy to support anything larger than the sumac and stunted cedar that were scattered around the clearing.

The deck itself was better built than the rest of the house, of Wolmanized two-by-eight planks surrounded by a heavy railing. A couple of folded aluminum lawn chairs were stacked against the wall, but I ignored them. Instead, I leaned against the railing, let the sun warm my face, and tried to decide what to do next.

They weren't at the beach house or here, and probably hadn't been. They owned roughly two hundred acres of hunting land, but I really couldn't see them roughing it in a lean-to back in the woods. Farnsworth's people had blundered around the place on quadra-trax, and while they were city boys and could easily have missed a camouflaged hideout, the Costas wouldn't have banked on that. Not on their own place, anyway. It was just too small to hide on. I was wondering whether I could con Bradleigh into sending me down to Bimini to look for them when I caught a glimpse of something at the edge of the meadow.

I had no sense of its shape or color, only movement. I was reaching inside my jacket for my mini-binoculars when I saw the wink of light against the dark of the forest, and then the railing exploded and a fist hammered me in the midsection.

I spun back into the wall from the force of the blow, falling, hearing the crack of the rifle as I slammed down on the deck. I was stunned, my wind gone. The gun roared again and one of the lawn chairs leapt crazily in the air and clattered down beside me. Hit or not, I had to get off the porch. Scrambling frantically across the deck to the open doorway, I launched myself through it as the glass door blew out beside me, spraying me with stinging fragments as I fell.

I rolled to my left until I banged into the bar and lay there gasping, trying to clear my head. My fingers fumbled over the wound in my belly but I couldn't tell how bad it was. It was numb and the vest was torn and full of splinters.

A slug ripped through the wall a few feet overhead, letting a shaft of sunlight into the room. Christ, he could shoot right through this crackerbox! I unzipped the blaze-orange vest, peeled it off and threw it across the open doorway. A slug punched through the paneling just above it, then another, six inches from the first. More sunlight was in the room now, beaming in through the bullet holes, glittering in the shattered glass on the floor.

I scrambled backwards like a crab along the bar. Breathing a silent prayer, I reached up and tugged on the latch of the gun safe door. And it swung open. I hadn't spun the combination dial when I closed it. I slid behind it and none too soon. A slug slimmed into it with a *punnnggg* that made it hum like a Chinese gong. But it didn't penetrate. Hell, it probably barely scratched the paint.

Sitting up with my back against the door, I pulled open my jacket and my shirt and looked down at the hole in my belly. Only there wasn't one. There was some blood, but not very much, nothing like the pulsing flow that spelled goodbye. I seemed to have a deep welt with a lot of splinters sticking out of it. It looked like I'd been rammed with the broken end of a baseball bat, which was probably close to the truth. The railing must have absorbed most of the impact of that first shot. Too bad the cabin wasn't built out of the same stuff.

I flinched as another bullet blew through the wall and *thwocked* into the paneling across the room, and then again as another slug *thunked* against the safe door. And I felt a rush of anger that surged up from my aching midsection to my fingertips.

Adrenaline. Combat Heat.

He was having a great time out there, plinking away at the cabin like I was a metal figure on a target range. And he could do it all damn day. Nobody would investigate gunfire this time of year.

I started to reach for my Beretta, then shook my head and grabbed the Enforcer carbine out of the rack. What the hell, I was sitting next to a survivalist's dream. I jacked a shell into the chamber and peered around the edge of the safe door. I couldn't return fire from here. I'd have to make it back to the doorway.

I waited until the next slug blew threw the opposite wall, then scrambled quickly to the door on my knees, and took a fast look. A gray haze of gun smoke was hanging in the air in front of a stand of birches across the meadow. I brought the enforcer up waist high and pulled the trigger. And pumped off fifteen rounds in the first burst. The carbine had been modified to fire full automatic! I fired two more long bursts, shouting over the roar of the gunfire, the Enforcer jumping in my hands with an angry life of its own.

The slide locked open, signaling an empty clip, and I risked the few seconds it took to jerk the banana clip out and reverse it. I released the bolt and opened fire again, hosing down the trees across the meadow with two long bursts. When the slide clanked empty the second time, I crawled quickly back behind the Treadlok door.

I grabbed one of the Ruger Mini-14's out of the rifle rack, checked the load, and waited for the return fire, panting, my eyes stinging from the powder smoke, the numbness in my belly beginning to change to a fiery ache. I took shallow breaths, trying to bring my breathing under control. And I waited. But there wasn't any return fire.

Maybe I'd gotten lucky and nailed him. I doubted it. Not

firing blindly from the hip at somebody eighty yards away in cover, no matter how many rounds I threw. He still had the advantage, his cover was better than mine and he could move around. But he'd also thought it was going to be easy, and that idea'd just been rudely erased. One minute he was out there banging happily away at a sitting duck, and suddenly the duck started shooting back with a machine gun.

Surprise, surprise.

He was moving. I knew it instinctively, probably because I knew I sure as hell would be. I crawled back to the shattered glass door and peered around the frame. Nothing. The sun was in my eyes, and there was too much smoke in the air. I could barely make out the hazy outlines of the trees across the meadow. And I couldn't go out this way. There was no cover on the deck at all.

I clambered through the debris back to the front door. I felt glass splinters bite into my elbows and knees, but I didn't get to my feet until I was outside with the house between me and the meadow. I circled around to the left and slid along the wall with my back pressed against the siding. And took a quick look.

There. I could see a faint cloud of powder smoke against the trees on the other side of the clearing. It was drifting slowly northward, pushed by the breeze. I tried to estimate how far it had moved. I couldn't be sure, but I could see the gouges and torn bark where I'd hosed down the trees. Close. Maybe I hadn't hit him, but I'd been very close. He was gone. He was hustling off through the underbrush just as fast as his legs could carry him, I'd bet my last dime on it.

But I wouldn't bet my life. And if I tried to make it across that meadow in the open, that's what I'd be doing. If he wasn't gone, then I would be before I'd traveled ten yards. No bet.

Sliding back away from the corner of the house, I moved into the trees that ringed the meadow. I stayed low, keeping as much cover between me and the open field as possible. I glanced out at the meadow when I could, but I was a lot more interested in the forest ahead of me. If whoever-it-was was really serious about taking me out, he might well be circling, too.

It was warm work. The brush near the house had been thinned out, but as I moved further into the woods, the going got rougher. The adrenaline started to wear off and my knees felt wobbly. And my midsection ached like it'd been chewed by a beaver with dull teeth.

It took no more than ten minutes to circle the meadow, but it seemed much longer. Years, in fact. And then I began to see the effects of machine gun fire, shattered branches, pock marks, rips in the bark of trees. Tommy guns do play hell with nature, but near misses don't count.

And then I found my first trace of him. A blaze-orange vest, similar to mine, lying on a stump. He'd probably parked it before he'd gotten into position. And either he'd left it behind, or he was nearby. I eased down on my belly and commando-crawled the rest of the way, the Mini-14 at the ready.

But he was gone.

I cut his trail first, broken leaves, scuffed earth, the marks a man leaves when he's running. I followed it for twenty or thirty yards on my belly, but my midsection ached too fiercely to stay down, and I knew it was unnecessary anyway. His tracks disappeared into the trees fifty or sixty yards away. He'd waited until I stopped firing and then beat feet, just as I'd thought. And I didn't blame him a bit.

I jogged along on his trail for a quarter mile or so until it ended suddenly at a fence beside a dirt road. A car had been parked here, but it was long gone now, and judging from the gouges in the gravel it had left in a hurry.

Which was just as well. My adrenaline rush was on a downhill slide and I didn't feel like tangling with anybody any bigger than Shirley Temple used to be.

I backtracked to the spot he'd fired from, a small grove of birches a few yards in from the edge of the meadow. It told me a little. It was open to the sky, which meant he'd probably followed me here as opposed to any kind of a permanent watch on the house. And I found a dozen empty cartridge cases and a couple of live rounds he'd apparently dropped when I opened up with the Enforcer. 30/06 military surplus steel-jacketed bullets. Not much good for hunting, but terrific for shooting through buildings, cars, or people. And the shooter was probably a man. The 30/06 packs quite a wallop. A woman *could* handle it, but would be more likely to pick something lighter.

I'd missed him. I'd banged up a lot of trees and maybe caused a coronary or two among the local wildlife, but I'd seen no trace of blood on his trail. Which is about the way the 'lotsa firepower' theory worked out in combat, too. I'm sure a defense department whiz kid could flummox me with a probability table, but the bottom line was; he had a rifle, and I had the machine gun, and he'd come closer to me than I had to him.

A lot closer.

I felt shaky, but I forced myself to follow my steps back to the lodge, keeping under cover all the way. Picked up the sniper's discarded orange vest to replace my own. Perfect fit. Again, probably a man. Who was a pretty fair shot.

I stopped for a moment on the deck to examine the railing.

It had been blown in half, and he'd missed me by no more than an inch or two. I'd been careless out here. And very lucky. And I'd probably used up my quota for the year.

I considered taking the Mini-14 or the Enforcer with me, but the penalty just for possessing a modified automatic weapon is something like twenty years, and I didn't think telling the cops 'it isn't really mine, I only stole it' would help my case much.

So in the end I put them both back in their respective racks in the safe, found a grocery bag in the kitchen and picked up most of the .30 caliber brass the Enforcer'd tossed around and put the bag in the safe also. Then I swung the steel Treadlok door closed. And this time I spun the combination dial.

Chapter

Twelve

It was nearly four when I parked the Mustang in front of my motel room. Easing out of the driver's seat, I walked down to number four-twenty-two. Stopped in front of it for a moment, listening to the murmur of the TV from within. I glanced casually around the deserted parking lot, then leaned back and kicked Lugo's door open.

Newspaper pages exploded into the air, fluttering to the floor as Enrique fumbled frantically under his pillow for . . . whatever. He stopped groping when he recognized me.

"Wake up, *hermano*," I said, "vacation's over."

He swung his legs over the side of the bed, his face darkening with anger. "What the fuck's wrong with you?" he said. "You could get your fuckin' head blown off pulling shit like that."

"Not as fast as I can get it blown off listening to you talk about what a soft deal I've got."

"What are you talking about, man?"

"Junior, maybe. Somebody tried to take me out up at the lodge this afternoon."

"Did you see him?"

"Not up close, no."

"What makes you think it was Junior then?"

I tossed one of the 30/06 cartridges to him and he snatched

it in mid-air. "Military surplus ammo," I said. "There's a bunch of it in the gun safe up there, along with some paramilitary weapons. I think Junior likes to play soldier."

"You got that part right," Lugo nodded, "he thinks he's Rambo or somethin'. He's a good shot though, how come he missed?"

"He didn't, exactly. But I'm a very lucky guy. Bulletproof almost. Something you might want to keep in mind."

"Nobody's bulletproof. And I never worry about luck one way or the other. What kind of a gun was it?"

"I don't know. A lot of military weapons use 30/06."

"No, I mean, was it an automatic or not?"

For a moment I was back in the lodge, pressed against the Treadlok door, flinching as the slugs ripped methodically through the wall, tasting the plaster dust. And the fear. "No," I said, "not an automatic. Too long between shots."

"Then it probably wasn't Rollie. He's got this thing about machine guns. He woulda used one."

"Maybe he doesn't want to risk carrying one around. They're illegal. Or hadn't you heard?"

"Yeah, I mighta heard that someplace. Except it don't mean squat. Rollie's got a license."

"A what?"

"A license, man, from the Treasury Department. Bradleigh fixed it up all legal. Rollie's never taken a fall for anything, so he got a license to deal firearms. That's his gig. I never used him myself, he's too flaky, but I guess he can get you anything from a blade to a bazooka. And he owns about a dozen machine guns. You sure he wasn't just takin' his time?"

"I'm sure. What about Roland?"

"Not likely. Roland wouldn't carry anything that'd mess up the fit of his suit, you know? Besides, he's got a bum shoulder. Had to be somebody else."

"Like who?"

"I don't know, but we must be buggin' 'em or they wouldna tried to take you down. I think I better make a coupla calls. Maybe he hired somebody I know and we can set up some kinda meet." He slipped into his black Gucci loafers, rolled his shirtsleeves down, and carefully buttoned his cuffs.

"Going somewhere?" I asked.

"I can't call from here. The cops know who I am, and there's only two fuckin' pay phones in this whole town. Too easy to bug. I'm gonna bop down to whatsisface—Laurance—make the calls from there."

"Sure that's far enough away? Laurance could be bugged too. Why not Toronto? They probably wouldn't think of that."

"Whaddya talkin' about, Toronto? You think I'm cuttin' out on you, Cruz?"

"No, no. I know you wouldn't run out on a brother, right? *Viva la Raza* and all that. Still, somebody who didn't know you might wonder. A guy sniffs a little gun smoke and drives forty miles to make a phone call."

"Think what you want," he said. "I'll be back later tonight. Unless somebody tells me otherwise."

"You can make your calls from Nome for all I care," I said. "I didn't want you in this in the first place."

"Yeah, well, I don't care much what you want. And don't be kickin' my door in again. Next time you could get killed."

"Hey, lighten up. What's a little joke between friends."

"You're crazy, you know that?"

"A little, maybe. You might want to keep that in mind, too."

"I don't think I'll lose much sleep over it."

"No reason you should," I said, "at least not back in Laurance. Have a nice trip, *hermano*."

"Fuck you, Cruz," he said.

Chapter

Thirteen

I stood in the shadows a moment outside Lugo's door, looking the parking lot over. A few cars had pulled in but nothing seemed suspicious. Still, I knew I was unpopular with somebody, so I lingered, trying to recapture the combat edge I'd felt up at the lodge, the sense of being wired, ultra-alert. Ready for Freddy.

There was a time, during Vietnam and when I'd gone on to the cops afterward, that I could call it up at will, just focus on it and it would come, an instant rush of intensity and anger. But not anymore. Now I only feel it when I'm actually in a jam, and maybe someday soon it won't come at all. And then I guess I'll have to find another line of work. Assuming I'm still around.

"Cruz?"

She called my name a second time before it registered. Rachel Graham had stepped out of the motel office and was staring at me oddly. Good thing I was combat-ready. I might have missed her altogether. And that would have been a pity. She'd added a touch of makeup around her eyes but her hair was still tied back in the ponytail. She was wearing a bulky peasant blouse of unbleached muslin with leather buttons over faded, fitted blue jeans and blue pumps. She looked like the middle sister, the one between the youngest and the oldest. And the best looking one in the family.

"What are you doing?" she asked.

"Practicing mental alertness," I said, "couldn't you tell? What are you doing?"

"Waiting for you, actually," she said, "I was hoping to talk to you before I go to work. Have you got a minute?"

"I've got all day. I'm on sort of a vacation, or so I've been told."

"You haven't lost your job or anything?" she said, concerned.

"No, in fact I was just telling my boss what a bang up time I've been having. He got a big kick out of it."

"Mr. Lugo's your boss?"

"For this week," I said. "What's up?"

"Oh, it's nothing really," she said uncertainly, looking very attractively flustered, "I just thought—no, never mind. It's silly, really."

"Silly would be good," I said. "I've been working hard all day providing yuks for other folks. I could use a little comic relief. So what's silly?"

"I'll have to show you," she said resignedly, "but you'll think it's juvenile, and you'll be right."

"I certainly hope so," I said, following her into the motel office. The door behind the counter was partly open and I could hear the eternal TV laugh track from beyond it. She closed it gently, then crossed to the other door at the end of the counter, took a key from her blouse, and opened it.

We were in an airy, open, one-room apartment. The room was done in shades of pastel green, richly patterned plush carpet, flocked wallpaper, a queen-sized bed with matching bedroom furniture at one end of the room, a comfortable sitting area around a wide bow-window that looked out into the forest on the other. I've never cared much for the color green in anything but plants, but as background for an auburn-haired lady, the room seemed exactly right.

"Very nice," I said, closing the door softly behind me.

"Thank you kind sir," she said, "one tries. Can I offer you something? A Beck's?"

"That would be terrific. It's been a long day."

"I thought you said you were on vacation," she said. She rummaged in the color-coordinated refrigerator, came up with an iced mug, popped the top on a bottle of Beck's and poured it expertly to an inch from the rim. A small stereo system beside the bow window accompanied her movements with Debussy.

"Do you, ah, always keep these on hand?" I said, accepting the cut-glass mug.

"No, not always," she said, meeting my gaze with a half smile.

"Then it'll taste even better. What's the surprise?"

"Oh, it's probably not much of a surprise. Do you remember inviting me to the Sugar Bowl the other night?"

"Sure. Sorry if it seemed crude. I gather your taste in music's changed a bit since the Bowl."

"Broadened," she said, "not changed. For instance . . . "
She switched the sound system to phonograph mode and carefully lowered the arm onto a 45 record. The speakers popped and hissed for a moment, and then a guitar and cowbell blasted into the room. Mitch Ryder and Detroit. Rock and Roll. First song of the night, every night at the Bowl.

And I almost blew it.

I was about to make some lame crack about golden oldies when I noticed her face, rapt, lost in the music. It was just a song to me, nostalgic, but just a song. It was much more than that to her.

I eased down on the arm of an overstuffed recliner and

125

watched her, feeling a bit like a voyeur. There were a couple of pictures on the end table beside the chair, of Rachel and a blonde, blue-eyed little girl about four years old. The photographs were badly done, out of focus perhaps, but before I could decide why, the record ended.

"Well," she said after a moment, "what do you think?"

"I haven't heard that in a very long time."

"I'm not surprised. I found this copy at a garage sale. I listen to it once in awhile when I need a lift."

"The past is a nice place to visit," I said, "but I wouldn't want to live there."

"No, I suppose not."

A second record slid down the spindle and began. Flutes, whispering a soft tempo. "Theme from a Summer Place," Percy Faith, last song of the night, lights coming slowly up, 'thank you ladies and gentlemen, drive safe on your way home and watch out for the boys in blue 'cause they'll be watchin' out for you . . .'

"Would you like to dance," I said, rising.

"I really have to go to work," she said doubtfully, but she didn't move away as I took her carefully in my arms.

We swayed together to the music, tentatively at first, then more smoothly as we found the proper stances. I'm not a good dancer. She made me seem very good indeed. The song faded away and we waited in silence for it to begin again, moving together to a rhythm of our own. And when the flutes returned we meshed with the music seamlessly, as though Percy was directing by following us. And maybe he was.

When the song ended the second time, she turned away from me, lifted the phonograph arm, and switched the music back to Debussy. I reached up and gently untied the ribbon in her hair, letting it fall loose and free, in scented waves.

"We're not children anymore," she said quietly.

"Thank God for that," I said, nuzzling the curve of her neck. "If you want me to stop . . ."

She didn't answer. She undid the leather buttons of the embroidered peasant blouse and I slid it from her shoulders. Her skin was fair, pale as porcelain with a light dusting of freckles across her shoulders. Her brassiere was black, in sharp contrast with her skin. I unhooked it with fingertips that were far from steady and she shrugged out of it, tossed it toward the chair and turned to me. We held a kiss, soul to soul, for a very long time. Her collarbones were fine and symmetrical and I traced their outline gently with my tongue, enveloped in the scent of her, tasting the faintest tang of salt from her skin. Her breasts were rounded mounds, lightly garnished with freckles, with aureoles as dark and inviting as her eyes.

We walked slowly to the bed together, helped each other out of the remainder of our clothing, and made love as smoothly as we'd danced. And we lost an hour. And then another.

I awakened entangled in the seafoam green covering of her bed. We'd been lying together, talking quietly about something, when the world had gone gradually golden and I awoke alone to the sound of the shower and Rachel's voice humming over it. I rolled over, yawned and stretched deliciously, and tried to sit up, which was a huge mistake. My midsection had stiffened up and I felt like a tackling dummy for the Chicago Bears.

Easing slowly upright, I slid myself gently back until my shoulders were against the velvet-tufted headboard. I massaged my bruised torso, wincing at my own touch. I noticed another picture of Rachel and the little girl on the nightstand, and I picked it up to see if it was better focused than the ones on the end table.

But it wasn't the picture that was out of focus. The images were clear and bright. It was the little girl. Her chubby smile was slack, and her eyes were vague and narrow, showing a hint of mongolism in the upswept corners. I carefully replaced the photograph on the nightstand.

Rachel came out of the bathroom, barefoot, wearing only her black panties and bra. She'd tied her hair firmly back with a silk ribbon.

"It's not polite to stare," she said. Did I detect a faint note of uncertainty? Probably. Welcome to the sexual revolution.

"Impolite, maybe," I said, "but short of locking myself in the closet, irresistible. You're a very good looking woman."

"Mmmmm," she said, stepping into a severe black skirt. She chose a pearl gray blouse that would have passed muster at a nunnery to complete the ensemble.

"Is something wrong?" I said.

"I don't know. That's quite a bruise on your midriff. Recent?"

"It's a long story."

"I'll bet it is. I imagine you know quite a few . . . long stories."

"Meaning . . . ?"

"We've known each other two days," she said evenly, facing me as she buttoned her blouse. "I know what you must be thinking. Of me, I mean."

"Things happen at their own pace. There aren't any hard and fast rules about how long they're supposed to take."

"Maybe not for you," she said, "but then you travel around quite a bit, don't you."

I swallowed my reply, afraid of making things worse. When in doubt, don't. We'd made love with surprising intensity and abandon. And if the lady found this upsetting in the aftermath, I could understand that. I felt a little shaky myself.

"If things have been happening too quickly, we can slow them down," I said. "Sometimes slower is better."

She stared at me a moment, then nodded, with a trace of a smile. "Sometimes it is," she agreed.

"Can we, ah, run again tomorrow morning?" I asked. "Maybe we'll have time to talk."

"That would be nice," she nodded. "I have to go. Be . . . discreet when you let yourself out. I imagine you're good at that in your line of work. I'll see you later."

"I certainly hope so," I said.

She closed the door softly behind her.

I lay there a moment, wondering whatever happened to wham-bam-thank-you-ma'am. The sexual revolution showed promise, but it left a fair number of casualties behind. I sighed, climbed out of bed, and wandered around picking up my clothes.

If the lady was complicated, so be it. She was worth it, and the only uncomplicated women are in cartoons anyway. And even there you've got Cathy and Brenda Starr.

Still, it would have been more fun to get dressed with that loose, warm, morning-after glow without the nagging sense of unease. I looked at the photograph on the nightstand again before I left. She really was a lovely little girl. And nothing is ever simple.

Chapter

Fourteen

Letting myself out discreetly was no problem; the motel office was deserted. Darkness had fallen during the hours with Rachel. I scanned the parking lot as I strolled back to my cabin. Lugo's space was vacant, but that wasn't surprising. It was a little early for him to be back. If he was coming back.

And there was something odd about my car. It wasn't quite level. Someone in the back seat? I moved toward it cautiously, my hand inside my jacket on the butt of the Model 92.

The car was empty. But the left rear tire was flat. I knelt beside it, running my fingertips over the sidewall until I felt it. A half-inch slit.

"Stay down, motherfucker, don't even breathe." The voice was barely a whisper behind me. He moved up quickly and I felt something press between my shoulder blades. And against my buttocks. His shins were touching me. Sloppy. Very sloppy. I was getting aced by an amateur.

"You carryin' a piece?" he hissed, running one hand over my jacket, "yeah, sure you are. Okay, just ease it out, real slow and hand it over. You fuck up and I'll cut your throat, man. Now—"

"Cut my—?" I grabbed his ankle with my right hand, jerking it forward and twisting it, dumping him backward. He came down hard on his shoulders, his breath *whoofing* out. I swept his knife wrist with my left hand, clamping it, and jammed my thumb into the base of his palm. The knife bounced off the side of the car.

And I almost hit him.

But I managed to stop the blow a half-inch from his chin. Christ, he was just a kid. I slapped him hard, open-handed, across the mouth.

"Hey, wait a minute," he wailed, "please, I—"

"Shut up you little creep!" I hauled him to his feet, twisting his arm up between his shoulder blades. "Not another word."

Scooping up his switchblade from the gravel, I manhandled him toward my room, holding him against the wall one-handed while I groped for my key. He was whimpering, which for some reason only made me angrier. I yanked the door open and pitched him headlong into the room. He bounced off the bed and landed in a heap beside it. Slamming the door behind me, I switched on the lights.

He huddled against the side of the bed, cringing, his chin tucked against his shoulder to avoid a blow.

And he wasn't just a kid. He was at least eighteen, possibly more. He was dark-haired with pallid skin, and finely structured, almost feminine features. Five-seven or so, he was so slender he probably didn't weigh much over a hundred pounds. He was wearing a shiny blue nylon jacket with lots of zippers, black jeans, and eighty-dollar black Reebok high-top tennis shoes. And at a glance, I guessed the shoes at size seven. With checkerboard patterned soles.

I patted him down. I didn't expect to find another weapon and I didn't but I'd already been careless enough for one day. Or a lifetime. I took his wallet from his hip pocket and flipped it open. His driver's license picture was lousy, but it was a match. He was Kenneth T. Cielli, twenty years old, with an Algoma address.

"Get up," I said.

"What are you gonna do?" he said, huddling tighter against the bed.

"I'm gonna kick your ass through the wall if you don't get up," I said reasonably.

"Okay, okay." He got up slowly and sat on the edge of the bed, massaging his right wrist.

"Take off your jacket and open your shirt," I said.

"What?"

"Just do it. Show me your right shoulder."

He reluctantly peeled off the jacket and unbuttoned his collarless black-on-charcoal satin shirt. He tugged it open to expose his shoulder with a hint of seductiveness that told me more than I'd wanted to know. His skin was almost translucent, a faint network of blue veins visible on the surface. There were no bruises on his shoulder. He hadn't fired a 30/06 rifle recently. Or ever, probably.

"Kenny?" I said, "is that what they call you?"

"I don't have to tell you nothin'," he said, rebuttoning his shirt.

"You're right," I said, "but you should. For one thing, I can haul your butt down to the jail and charge you with attempted assault and armed robbery."

"You can't prove anything. There weren't no witnesses. It'd just be your word against mine. I know my rights."

"Right again," I agreed, "but I can also tell 'em you're the clown who trashed the Costas' beach house and lodge. Maybe I can't prove that either, but I don't think the Costas will care much about proof. Fairly basic folks, from what I hear."

"Jesus, you can't do that. They'll kill me."

"Probably," I said, "but that's not my problem."

"Look, I only wanted to talk to you, is all."

"About what? The contents of my wallet?"

"No, man, about Rol Junior. Heard you were lookin' for 'im. Well, I been lookin' for him too."

"At the beach house?" I said, "and the lodge?" He nodded, swallowing.

"Why are you looking for him?"

"Money, man, Rollie owes me."

"You made a helluva mess for somebody who was just looking for a few bucks."

"Maybe. I had my reasons."

"What reasons? Why does he owe you money?"

"He just does, man. He fucked me up and he's gotta pay for it."

"Okay, so Rollie owes you," I sighed. "What do you want from me?"

"You're lookin' for 'em, right? Somebody's payin' you to look?"

I nodded. "So?"

"So I know where they are, man. I can tell you. If we can do a deal."

I stared at him for a moment. What a thoroughly unlovely little bastard you are, I thought. "No," I said, "I don't think we can do a deal."

"What do you mean? Why not?"

"Because you don't know anything. You didn't just search the houses, you trashed 'em, because you think you've got a beef with Rollie. If you knew where he was, you wouldn't be putzing around with his furniture. You'd be trying to take him. The way you tried with me."

"Look, I can tell ya about this place they got near here. A hideout, like."

"What kind of a hideout?"

"Uh-uh." He shook his head. "Not for free, man. Nothin's for free."

"Come on, Kenny, do I look like I just fell off a turnip truck? You try to stick me up, blow that, and now you're tryin' a hustle. Gimme a break."

"No, it's true. I been there."

"You've been where?"

"Look, I gotta get somethin' outa this, Cruz. I can't make it up here no more. You gotta give me somethin'."

"If you think I'm going to pay you for some cockamamie story about a hideout, you're out of your tree, pal."

"What if I can prove I been there?"'

"All right, I'll tell you what. You tell me what you know about this hideout, straight, no snow, and if I believe it, I'll pay you. I give you my word."

"Your word," he snorted, "you gotta be kiddin'."

"You know, I'll bet Leo Buscaglia would beat the living crap out of you after a two-minute conversation."

"Who's Leo Bus—?"

"It doesn't matter," I said, cutting him off, "the bottom line is, I'll pay for your song and dance and nobody else will. And if I drop a dime on you about the beach house and the lodge, you're gonna need a skateboard and crutches to make it to the john. Now either give me what you've got or hit the door. I've had a long day."

He frowned, chewing on a cuticle while he thought it over. His fingernails were too long, with a layer of grime under them. I reminded myself that somewhere he had a mom who didn't think he was such a bad guy. Maybe.

"Well?" I said.

"Okay," he nodded grudgingly, "but you'll pay me, right?"

"If I believe you. Go ahead."

"All right, Rollie's got a place, a hideout, like a real fancy bomb shelter, or somethin'."

"Why do you say bomb shelter?"

"It didn't have no windows in it. But they had everything else in there, man, beds, guns, a TV. Enough food for a fuckin' army."

"How big a place is it?"

"It's like a one-room apartment, I guess, but pretty big. It's got a bathroom with a shower. Room enough for three or four people, you know?"

"Where is this place?"

"Well, I don't know, exactly, but—"

"Somehow I didn't think you would."

"No, no, I'm tellin' you true, man. I was stoned out of my gourd when Rollie took me out there."

"How long did it take to get there?"

"No more than a hour. And the roads were pretty bad. We even hadda change cars once."

"You noticed a lot for somebody who was stoned."

"That was on the way back, man. I wasn't stoned on the way back. But I couldn't see nothin'. They put this sack over my head, and—"

"They?"

"Rollie and his friend, the older guy."

"Not Roland Senior?"

"No, no. I know Rollie's dad. This was another guy, older'n Rollie but not like his dad. Your age, maybe."

"Mmmm," I said. "Look, why don't we just take this from the top. When did Rollie take you out there?"

"August, man, or maybe the first week in September. Rollie and me, we hang out together. He's always got dope and shit, and ah—well, I'm like a gigolo, you know? I pick up broads and sometimes Rollie likes to watch, so—"

"Kid," I said gently, "I know the kind of stuff Rollie's into, and I can guess what you're into, so let's just leave the ladies out of it, okay? Just tell me what happened."

He searched my face intently for a moment, looking for condemnation? Acceptance? I don't know. I tried to keep my expression neutral.

"Okay," he said, "okay. I peddle my ass sometimes. There ain't no other way I can make it up here. I ain't big enough to work in the woods, and—"

"A man's gotta do what a man's gotta do," I said, "so you and Rollie are buddies, and he pays sometimes, right?"

"Yeah, he pays, or he's got drugs, man, good stuff, not the kinda shit they got up here. Only this one time, he gives me some coke, and I snort it, but don't get no rush. I zonk out."

"You couldn't tell it wasn't coke?"

"I was already half blown away, man. It coulda been Drano for all I knew. Anyway, I wake up in this . . . place. With Rollie and the other guy. And I say hey, man, like I don't do parties, you know? And Rollie says it don't matter what I want, I can scream if I want, nobody'll hear me, and nobody knows where we are. We can stay forever if we want. Nobody'll find us out here."

"How long did you stay?"

"Three days, I think. They kept me handcuffed to this bed mosta the time, takin' turns on me, and then sometimes we'd do a manwich, or around the—"

"I get the picture," I interrupted, "tell me about the place. Do you have any idea where it was?"

"No, but it took us about a hour to get back. We rode in a jeep for the first part of it, then they put me in Rollie's car for the resta the way. I figure it was out in the woods someplace."

"That's not much help," I said, "you can cover a lot of

ground in an hour. Tell me more about the house."

"There ain't much more I can tell ya, it was big, there was this big rack of guns on one wall, tommy guns and stuff, it, ah, it had like a walk-in freezer off the kitchen. Rollie said we coulda stayed there forever and I believed him, man."

"What else?"

"I think the place mighta been underground. It didn't have no windows for one thing, but it was more'n that. I never heard anything while we was there, not a plane or a truck. Nothin'. Even back in the woods I shoulda heard somethin'. And I couldn't tell when it was daytime. It never got no warmer or colder. I just got the feelin' it was underground."

"Still not much help. What about Rollie's friend—did he have a name?"

"Rollie called him a lotta things, just kiddin' around, you know?"

"What kind of things?"

"Ah—Bear. He called him Pooh Bear sometimes, and Leo the Lion, and Tigger."

"Jesus H. Christ," I said softly.

"Yeah, I thought so too," Kenny nodded, "pretty weird, hunh."

"What did the friend look like?"

"Hung, man, really hung. That's why I said no parties at first, because—"

"Kenny, I meant what did his *face* look like."

"Oh, yeah, I see what you mean. Well, he was an older guy, thirty or forty maybe. Big guy, not fat, but big, like a football player, you know? Brown hair, fairly short but cut nice, styled. Had some gray in it by his ears. His body hair was partly gray too. Grossed me out, man."

"How tall was he?" I sighed.

"Not as tall as you. Five ten or eleven, I guess. He . . .

looked like a rich guy, somehow, you know? Classy? Even without no clothes on."

"Right. A very classy guy."

"He *was,* man, it's hard to explain but—I don't know, he talked right, you know? Like a butler in a movie or somethin'."

"You know, your whole story sounds a little like a movie to me. You haven't given me anything solid. An underground house, Leo the Lion and Tigger—"

"But it's true, man! I can prove it!"

"How can you prove it if you don't know where it is?"

"They were gonna kill me, man! I mean they talked about it with me right there. Rollie said they could off me and nobody'd find me in a thousand fuckin' years!"

"So why didn't they?"

"They didn't want no heat from Rollie's old man. Rollie was all hot to do it but the other guy talked him out of it. Said Roland'd kill 'em if he found out. Said they went to too much trouble buildin' the place to risk it over nothin'. He meant *me,* man, like I was nothin'."

I didn't say anything.

"So they just made sure I wouldn't talk. Lookit, man, lookit this!"

He tore open the black satin shirt and peeled it off. The skin on his back was crisscrossed with purplish welts, permanent scars from a brutal beating, and pocked with cigarette burns. "And this too, man! Lookit!" he screeched. He pulled his slacks down to his knees. His buttocks were scarred too, but that wasn't the worst of it. He'd been branded. An ugly keloid *R* four inches high had been burned into his left cheek.

"Okay," I said tightly, "I believe you. Get dressed."

Kenny didn't respond. He was staring at me intently, his eyes glittering expectantly. And he was getting an erection.

I turned away and stumbled to the bathroom, tasting the sour rush of bile in the back of my throat. I leaned my head over the sink and turned on the tap, swallowing rapidly, gripping the porcelain tightly with both hands. Nothing came up. I stood there awhile, listening to the rush of the water, trying not to think of anything in particular.

But one thought wouldn't pass.

I was going to find those bastards. All of them. And not for Lugo or Bradleigh, or the punk in the other room. For me. I'd find them for me.

The nausea passed, and still I stood there, staring down into the clear water swirling in the basin. It seemed like I'd been looking into the water for a very long time, but it was probably only a few minutes.

"Hey," Kenny called, "are you okay?"

I didn't answer at first. I took a deep breath and turned off the tap. The room seemed very quiet without the rush of the water.

"Hey, man, you can come out. I won't hurt you."

"Right," I sighed, shaking my head.

He was fully dressed, wearing the multi-zippered satin jacket and an expression of amused contempt. "How about the money, Cruz?" he said, rubbing his thumb and fingertips together in the universal mime. "You promised you'd pay me."

Money was good. I could talk about money. If he'd said anything else I think I might have beaten him half to death.

"The money's at the beach house," I said, "in the safe. Three hundred dollars."

"But I couldn't open the safe, man, it—"

"It's open now," I said, "I popped the lock. The cops know the place has been hit, though. You'll have to be careful."

"Three hundred bucks ain't much, man, after what they done."

"You're right," I agreed, "it's not, but that's all there is. Take it or leave it."

"I guess I got no choice. In the safe, right?"

"Right. You can leave as soon as you finish."

"Finish? What do you mean, man? Finish what?"

"Finish changing the tire on my car," I said, tossing him the keys. He caught them in mid-air. Our eyes met and held. "And don't even think about running," I said.

"No," he muttered, looking away. "No problem. I'll take care of it."

"Right," I said. "I'd appreciate it."

Chapter

Fifteen

After the kid left I stripped off my clothes and took a long shower. A very long shower. I've seen some funky things in my life, necklaces of human ears and heads mounted on poles in Vietnam. During my hitch as a cop I'd rolled on a family dispute that was settled with a machete, and another with a bicycle chain. But none of those things left a nastier aftertaste than that brand. The casual brutality of it offended my sense of . . . I don't know, propriety? Honor? I don't have a rock-solid personal code of conduct. There are things I will do and things I won't, and those things may vary according to the situation. There are injustices I can walk away from without a backward glance, and have, and there are those I have to do something about. And I'd just seen one.

I winced as I toweled off. My midsection was stiff and the bruise below my diaphragm was turning a lovely, angry purple. I also realized I was starving. A plate of Tubby's specialty of the house? And perhaps a smile from a maiden fair? Such a deal.

I dressed quickly and casually, clean jeans, a navy blue L.L. Bean chamois shirt, wool socks and Top-Siders. I thought about leaving the gun behind, carrying it meant I'd have to keep my jacket on through dinner, but in the end I strapped on the rig. I could still taste the plaster dust from the lodge.

I slipped on my windbreaker and stepped into the night. The temperature had fallen into the upper twenties and the wind was sharp and bitter, stinging my ears and cheeks. No snow yet, but soon. Lugo's parking space was still empty, and it was the only one in the lot. The week-enders had arrived and I pitied any buck without a place to hide in the morning. I left the Mustang where it was, wearing its spare, and jogged across the highway to the restaurant.

I spotted Lugo's Cadillac parked near the front door. Interesting. Tubby's was packed, a fifty-fifty mix of locals on their Friday night out, and red-suited invaders from the south. The noise and smoke hit me like a blow as I entered and for a moment I debated passing up supper. My stomach cast the deciding vote. No food, no strength for the morning run. Or whatever.

I pushed through the crowd looking for an empty table, and spotted one immediately. Sort of. Most of the tables were taken, many being shared by strangers, but Lugo was sitting alone at a table for four, calmly working on a platter of steak and hash browns. His overcoat was resting carelessly over the back of one of the chairs, but there was an air of territoriality about his stance that said *Do Not Disturb the Animals While Feeding* as clearly as a neon sign.

I shouldered through the crush to his table and sat down. He glanced up at me briefly, grunted, and continued masticating his steak.

"Nice to see you, too," I said.

He swallowed and took a long pull from a pilsner glass of ale, leaving a line of foam along his upper lip. "Bradleigh says it had to be one of them that tried to do you at the lodge. They got no other people up here he knows of."

"Wrong. They've got a friend, or at least Rollie does. And they've got a hideout, probably somewhere up in the hills, stocked with enough supplies to last a year."

Frowning, Lugo cut off a bloody piece of nearly raw steak, and speared it with his knife. "How'd you come by that? You sure about it?"

"How I learned it is none of your business, and no, I'm not sure."

"Any idea where this place is at?" he mumbled around a mouthful of meat.

"Not yet. It can't be on their land, though. Two hundred acres would be too easy to search. I'm guessing it's on a piece of private land owned by Rollie's buddy."

"This buddy got a name?"

"A few. Tigger, Pooh Bear, and . . . oh yeah, Leo the Lion."

Lugo scowled, searching my face. It was not a comfortable feeling. "Don't fuck around with me, Cruz. I ain't in the mood."

"Those are the names Rollie called him."

"You sayin' Rollie's asshole buddies with this guy? He's a fag?"

"Being gay is probably the least of Rollie's problems."

"Not when Eladio finds out about it. He's an old-fashioned guy, Eladio. This could change things."

"How do you mean?"

"We might have to hit 'em," Lugo shrugged. "It's a rule, no junkies, no fags. Too undependable."

"Then you'd better not tell him about it. I'll have no part of that."

"Look, you don't understand. Bradleigh wanted to send more people up here and I told him we'd handle it. I can't call him back'n ask for help now without lookin' like a jerk. We gotta handle this ourselves."

"Fine. Then just pretend you didn't hear the part about

Rollie's sex life, because if I even *think* you want to do any-thing but talk to the Costas, I'm gonna walk. And you haven't got prayer one of finding them on your own."

"What the fuck you care what happens to 'em?" he said. "Christ, they were shootin' at you this morning. You should want 'em taken out."

"Maybe, but not like this. If I have to take somebody down defending myself I will, but I won't set them up for a hit, and it's my way or the highway on this. So what's it gonna be?"

He shook his head slowly. "Okay, okay," he conceded, "so I don't talk to anybody about Rollie. Yet. But you're makin' a mistake buckin' me, Cruz. I've whacked guys for a lot less. When this is over you'n me could have serious problems."

"I don't think so, Enrique. You're not stupid, and trying to take me out would be a stupid move."

"Yeah? Why's that? You don't think I could do it?"

"Maybe so, maybe not. Nothing's certain in this life. Maybe we'd both get hurt. And the thing is, neither one of us would get paid for it."

He eyed me for a moment, mulling that over, then shrugged and hacked off another piece of meat. "Maybe it'd be worth it. So what do we do now?"

"We stay visible. We spooked them this morning. They tried me and came up empty. Maybe they'll contact you now."

"Or maybe they'll try to take you out again," Lugo smiled, chewing. It was not a pretty sight.

"I was careless this morning. Somebody told me I was on vacation up here and I believed it. That won't happen again. Enjoy your meal, Enrique, I'll see you around."

A small booth against the opposite wall had emptied and I pushed through the crowd to it. I was starving, but I wasn't hungry enough to share a table with Lugo. When he finished his steak he'd probably crack the bones between his teeth and lick the platter clean. Or at least that's what I told myself. I think what really made me uneasy around him was that we were too much alike. If a few things had happened differently in my life, I might've turned out like him. And I still might.

I'd only caught glimpses of Rachel moving briskly through the crush, escorting diners to tables and waitresses to diners, but I'd barely settled myself when she was there, gathering the dirty dishes onto a tray. Which was just as well since I'd been eyeing the remains of a slightly used sandwich.

"Hi," I said, "where is everybody tonight?"

"We cater to a select clientele. Most of them are even wearing shoes. What would you like?"

"Something edible and something wet. Not necessarily in that order."

"Gosh, a gourmet. We don't get many up here. I recommend the muskrat livers on a buffalo chip."

"Fine, bring me six and have one for yourself."

"Oh, I never eat here. I've seen the kitchen." She smiled and disappeared into the crowd. I swiveled slowly in my seat to watch her go. The bush-hat party was in residence at their usual table. One of them reached for Rachel as she passed but she avoided the grab with a deft sideslip that left him pawing the air . . .

Something clanked on my table. A thin strand of beaten gold was sitting in the ashtray, and Hec Michaud, the beer drinker from the cemetery, had slid into the booth opposite me.

"You lost that out to the cemetery," he said, "I figured you'd want it back." He was clutching a can of Blatz in his left fist instead of generic beer, but that was the only thing changed from the morning. He was still wearing the greasy coveralls and I could smell the rancid odor of stale sweat and beer breath across the table. His eyes were slightly glazed and I guessed that he'd been drinking steadily all day. I picked the bracelet carefully out of the ashtray.

"I didn't lose this," I said mildly. "I gave it to Paulie. It's kind of a—"

"I know what it is. It's a reminder he got his fuckin' brains scrambled. Well he don't need no reminder, see, and neither do I. He ain't a bad worker mosta the time. He's a little smarter'n a backhoe and he don't mind gettin' down in the holes to square 'em off, but he ain't right in the head. He walks around talkin' to the stiffs and moonin' about his old buddies, which is all he's been doin' since you give him this fuckin' hunka wire. So you take it back. And take your chilibean ass back to Detroit where you belong."

Reflex. I grabbed the front of his overalls and jerked him over the table in less time than it took to think it. "Why don't we discuss this outside," I said reasonably.

He didn't pull back. His eyes were only inches from mine but he didn't flinch. "We can go outside," he hissed, "maybe you can even whip my ass. I ain't no hot shot sojer-boy, I'm just a workin' stiff tryna get by. But I'll tell you somethin' Cruz, you'll be gone in awhile maybe, but Paulie won't. He'll still be workin' for me. And if he ain't then he'll be sittin' on the fuckin' porch at the county home, cause nobody else'll have 'im, see? So you'n me can go outside'n dance, but Paulie'll be the one payin' the fiddler, understand? He'll be the one payin'."

I almost hit him anyway. It was a near thing. I held his coveralls knotted in my fist so tightly my arm was humming like a power line. But I didn't hit him. I pushed him gently back into his seat, and smoothed the front of his bibs with my fingertips.

"I think you'd better go," I said, surprised at how calm I sounded.

"Yeah," he said, stumbling to his feet, "I'll go back to the bar, and you go back to beantown, Cruz. Leave us alone."

"You've made you're point, Hec," I said, "don't push it."

He snorted, tossed off the remainder of his beer with one long pull and banged the empty can down on my table, spraying me with flecks of foam. And I still managed not to hit him somehow. But it was hard not to. It was very, very hard.

He swaggered back to his place at the bar. Next to Paulie. Funny, I hadn't noticed him before, but Paulie was standing at the bar, staring at me over the heads of the crowd, his expression neutral, unreadable. Then Hec said something to him and slapped him on the shoulder and he turned away.

Rachel arrived with my supper a few minutes later, beef tips on a bed of wild rice and an iced pilsner of Beck's. I glanced at it, surprised. I'd almost forgotten I was hungry.

"Muskrat livers," she announced, placing the platter on the table with a flourish, "and a tall cool one. Rather like yourself, in fact."

"Thank you. For the food and the kind words."

"Something wrong?" she said, frowning.

"Wrong? What are you, a witch?"

"No, but I noticed Hec Michaud over here, and your mood's cooled about ten degrees. Did he say anything? To upset you, I mean?"

"No, he just wanted to give me my bracelet back." I picked up the wrist wire and spun it on my index finger.

"If I'd known you were engaged I would never have—on second thought, maybe I would have anyway." She arranged the silverware quickly and expertly.

"We're not engaged," I said. "It's a long story. I'd be

happy to bore you with it later."

"Maybe tomorrow," she said. "I won't get off until midnight and I'll be whipped. And I had a very busy afternoon."

"Me too," I said. "Can I chase you into the forest tomorrow morning, do you think?"

"If you think you can keep up." She reached out, brushing my cheek with the side of her index finger. "Gotta go," she said, and was off into the crowd.

The beef tips were delicious, lightly glazed with a tart and smoky sauce. The wild rice was crisp and steaming and the Beck's was icy smooth. I noted all of these things like a eunuch at a triple-X film festival, with admiration, but not much enjoyment. Mostly I watched Hec and Paulie at the bar. Hec consumed four or five beers while carrying on a nonstop noisy critique of the taped football game on TV. Paulie nursed a single glass, ignoring the game, ignored by the people around him, alone in the crowd.

It took longer than I expected, but eventually Hec moved off unsteadily toward the men's room. I got up and made my way to the vacant space at the bar.

"Hello, Paulie," I said, "How's it going?"

"Hey, Flower," he grinned, "good. I'm good." But the easy smile faded and he looked uncomfortable.

"Look," I said carefully, "I understand your situation and I don't want to cause trouble for you, but, well, I still want you to have this thing—"

"No. No, you better keep it, Flower," he said, shaking his head. "Hec don't like me wearin' it. He's a jerk sometimes, but he ain't a bad guy, and I gotta work for 'im, you know?"

"So don't wear it," I said, "just take it. You must have a place you can keep it, right?"

"Yeah," he said, nodding slowly, his smile returning,

"yeah, I guess I could do that. Maybe I can wear it Saturdays when Hec don't work. That'd be okay, wouldn't it?"

"I think so," I said. "I'd better get back. Take care of yourself."

"Right . . . Hey look, Flower, thanks a lot. I really appreciate your takin' the trouble and all."

"That's all right," I said, "I'll see you around, Paulie."

"Yeah," he nodded, "see ya." He stared at the thin gold bracelet for a moment, then furtively slipped it into the vest pocket of his work shirt.

I was making my way back to my booth when there was a roar from the crowd near the jukebox. Something was happening with the bush-hat party. They were standing around their table, nearly a dozen of them, clad in various combinations of hunting togs and sports clothes, cheering and whooping. I thought for a moment bush-hat had found another sucker to pound on, but then I caught a glimpse of auburn hair and a black skirt, and I realized bush-hat was holding Rachel on his lap. I couldn't see what was going on, but the whistles and catcalls told me all I needed to know.

I tried to keep the lid on as I pushed through the crush, going in angry is foolhardy, but there were too many people in my way, and when a second roar went up I started shoving gawkers aside as though I was still wearing a badge and a blue suit.

Bush-hat was sitting at his table, drenched and sputtering, wiping beer off his face with one hand, holding Rachel's wrist with the other. She was standing calmly beside him, holding the empty pitcher of beer she'd just dumped on him. Good for her.

"Let her go," I said. Bush-hat looked up at me, surprised.

"Cruz, it's all right," Rachel said, "I can—"

"I said let her go, Fats. Do it now."

"Hey buddy," a guy on my right said, grabbing my shoulder, "why'n't you—"

I slapped him hard in the privates. He sucked wind, hunching over from the instant agony, and I clubbed him to the floor with an elbow to the temple. He went down like a sack of cement.

"Hoo-eee!" Bush-hat yelled, grinning, "what we got here?" He pushed Rachel aside, groping at her breasts as she stumbled away, and I forgot every scrap of combat training I've ever had and dove at him across the table, tackling him chest high, carrying him over backwards.

We hit the floor hard, tangled with his chair and with each other, squirming, grunting as we exchanged short, furious blows. He was quicker than I'd expected. He jammed his fingertips up into my left armpit trying to roll me off. It felt like somebody was trying to pry my arm off with a spade, and I went over, slamming my head on a chair leg. I caught a glimpse of a blur coming from my right and managed to tuck my head to avoid a kick, but I couldn't duck the second boot. It slammed into my midsection and broke me in half.

My breath *whooshed* and everything disappeared in a sheet of white agony. Bush-hat caught me with a right hand shot to the upper jaw that would have taken my head off if it had landed squarely. He managed to get his thigh over my waist and push himself upright, sitting on my waist, raining punches down on me, grunting with each swing. I was catching most of the blows on my forearms, operating on pure reflex, but it was only a matter of time till I missed one and he'd hand me my head.

And then Paulie elbowed through the ring of gawkers. Two of bush-hat's buddies tried to grab him and he casually demolished them both with combat judo, catching one with an ankle sweep that dumped him over the table and the other across the bridge of the nose with a back-fist, hammering him into the crowd like he'd been pole-axed. He grabbed bush-hat by the back of the collar and hauled him off me.

"Come on," he said, irritated, "let him up. This ain't no way to behave."

I managed to get to my knees, trying to breathe. "Paulie," I squeaked, but it was too late. Somebody clobbered him from behind with a beer pitcher and his knees went rubbery and he toppled like a tree and disappeared beneath a mob of red suits and flannel shirts.

Bush-hat hunched into a sparring stance, his ham-sized fists moving in front of him, his feet shuffling a little. Apparently he was a boxer of sorts. And a sportsman. He gave me a moment to get to my feet before he waded in and uncorked a wide, looping haymaker at my head. I slipped the punch, grabbing his wrist as it whistled past my face, pulled him toward me and kicked him hard under the ribcage. He went white, gasping, and I hit him with a quick combination to the same spot, doubling him over, then hammered him down with a forearm smash that caught him just below the right ear. Somebody grabbed me from behind, pinning my arms in a bear hug. I was groping for his groin when somebody screamed, a shriek of pure terror, and everything stopped.

"*Okay, that's it!*" Lugo roared. "*Nobody moves or I cut his fuckin' eyes out!*" He had one of Bush-hat's friends clamped in a chokehold, with a broken beer bottle jammed against the guy's forehead. A thin crimson stream was trickling into his eyes.

"Jesus, Jesus," the hostage pleaded, "please—"

"You!" Lugo snarled, "you let him go. *Now, Goddammit!*"

I stumbled forward, freed from the bear hug. I hauled a short, pudgy character in a blue flannel shirt away from Paulie. He was on his hands and knees, and the back of his head was a mat of blood and foam from the shattered pitcher.

He looked up at me, dazed. "Mom?" he said.

"Come on," I said, "get up, Paulie. Come on."

"All right, what's the problem?" Clint Mattis was bulling his way through the crowd, using his nightstick to clear a path. Lugo casually dropped the broken bottle, crunching it under his heel, and pushed his hostage away from him. He was fading back into the crowd when Mattis said "Hold it, mister. Everybody stays put. Now what the hell's going on?"

"The guy in the suit had a busted bottle," Lugo's hostage sobbed, "he was tryna blind me."

"I don't see no bottle," Lugo shrugged, "it was just a scuffle, that's all. Anybody else see a bottle?" He glanced around the crowd, his eyes resting momentarily on each face. "Anybody see anything?" There was some muttering and foot shuffling from the spectators, but nobody said a word. And I didn't blame them. I helped Paulie to his feet. He still didn't seem to know me.

"Rachel," Mattis said, "what happened?"

"I don't know," she said, glancing at me, her face expressionless. "I imagine it was the usual kid stuff. A lot of noise about nothing."

"This looks like more than a push-and-shove to me," Mattis said. "Anybody want to file a complaint? It don't matter who started it, you got the right to file. How about you, mister?" he said to Lugo's hostage. The man shook his head mutely and turned away.

"All right then, let's break it up!" Mattis said, "show's over. Everybody either sit down or hit the door."

The crowd began to disperse and Lugo disappeared into it. A couple of Bush-hat's friends tried to help him up but he couldn't quite make it. He sat on the floor, glancing around wearing a numb smile. I felt no particular antipathy toward him now. He was a jerk, but he'd let me get to my feet when he didn't have to, an honorable thing to do, if not very bright.

"Get the fuck away from him!" Hec Michaud said, shouldering me roughly aside, taking Paulie's arm. "You satisfied now you got the rest of his brains knocked out?"

I reached for him but Mattis stepped between us. "Get the dummy outa here, Hec, he's bleedin' all over the place. Go get him sewed up. Cruz, I knew you were gonna be trouble, I just knew it. You were right in the middle of this, weren't ya?"

"A lot of people were in it," I said mildly. Hec lead Paulie toward the front door, dazed and stumbling.

"He didn't start it, Clint," Rachel sighed. "He was in a booth by the wall."

"Yeah? So who did start it, Rache?"

"An overgrown kid," she said evenly, "he's already gone."

"Yeah, well, since he was obviously a participant, I think I'll just escort Mr. Cruz here, out. You got any objection to that, Mrs. Graham?"

"None at all," she said, "just make sure he pays his bill first."

Chapter

Sixteen

The icy air of the parking lot cut into my battered lungs like a dull bread knife. I tried to keep my breathing shallow to ease the sting.

"Where's your car?" Mattis said.

"Across the street," I said, my voice barely above a whisper. My chest felt like a keg full of broken bones and shattered glass.

"All right, why don't you just walk over there, pack your gear and hat up. I've had it with you clowns, Cruz. You come crossways of me one more time and you're gonna think what happened in there tonight was a tea dance."

"Mattis," I sighed, "I've got business here, and I'm over twenty-one, and I'm not going anyplace. If you've got a problem with that, why don't we just settle it right now, one way or the other."

"Settle it?" he snorted, "mister, I got my doubts you can make it across the road without help."

"Maybe not," I conceded, "that's my problem. What about yours?"

He stared at me a moment, then shrugged. "My problem is guys like you, Cruz. Come into a little town, throw your money around, push people. So you're from Detroit. Big fuckin' deal. If we wanted to live down there we could find it, you know. Wouldn't need a map, either, just head south till you see a lotta smoke and a lotta spooks. You ain't no better'n us Cruz, you just think you are."

"What I think is, you've got an inferiority complex, Mattis, only in your case it's probably justified. Maybe you should try to get a little help."

"You just remember what I told you, city boy, or you're the one's gonna be needin' the help."

He turned and stalked off to his patrol car, his boots crunching in the icy gravel of the parking lot. He climbed in, cranked it up, and roared out on the highway, spraying me with dust and stone chips. Nice fella.

He was right about one thing, though. I had my doubts I could make it back to my room without a couple of medics and a stretcher. I tried a couple of tentative steps. As long as I didn't try to walk and breathe at the same time . . .

"My God," Rachel said quietly, "if it isn't the Lone Ranger. And without his horse. Can you walk?"

"Of course I can. I was just waiting to escort you across the highway, ma'am."

"I don't need any help crossing the highway," she said, "and I didn't need any help in there either. He was just a drunk, Cruz. It's not high on my list of fun things to do, but I'm perfectly capable of handling an occasional drunk, and I would have, if you hadn't butted in. There was no reason for anyone to get hurt. It was stupid and unnecessary."

"You're probably right," I admitted. "Still, when I have to face Randolph Scott in that giant saloon in the sky, what am I supposed to say? Gee, Mr. Scott, I figured she could handle that big palooka on her own?"

"I'm serious."

"Okay then, seriously, didn't your little heart go pitty-pat just a teensy bit faster when I came blundering to your rescue.

155

Come on, 'fess up. Didn't it?"

"God, you're hopeless."

"You're right," I said, "and I'm also damn near helpless. Do you suppose you could flag down traffic long enough for me to crawl across the road?"

"Are you still joking or are you really hurt?"

"I'm not sure," I said, "maybe both."

"If I had any sense I'd just go back inside and leave you here to die."

"If you had any sense that's exactly what you should do," I agreed.

"Come on," she sighed, "there's a first aid kit in the motel office."

"Shouldn't you tell someone at the restaurant . . . ?"

"I've already told Tubby I was leaving early. But don't read anything heavy into that."

"Nope," I said, "of course not."

Rachel collected a white metal first aid kit from behind the office counter and let us into her apartment.

"Have a seat at the kitchen table," she said briskly, "I'll get an ice pack for your jaw before it swells any more."

"Gee, I feel pretty wobbly, maybe I should lay down on the bed."

"You're not staying, Cruz. I'll patch you up out of pity, but after that you're on your way."

"Really? I thought you were scheming to take advantage of me in my weakened condition."

"Dream on," she said, "and in the meantime, sit." She gathered a handful of ice cubes from the refrigerator, wrapped them in a hand towel and crushed them with a steak mallet. "Are your teeth all right?"

"They seem to be," I said, clicking them together as best I

could. The hinge on my jaw seemed to be torqued one notch too tightly.

"Good," she said, "you have a nice smile. Hold this against your jaw." She handed me the ice pack. "Where else are you hurt?"

"All kidding aside, no place that I can't handle myself if you want me to go."

"Not a chance," she said, "I'm enjoying this. And if you're not hurt as badly as you deserve, I may give you a few more whacks myself. You're wincing when you talk. Your ribs?"

"They hurt a little," I admitted. "Are you a nurse on top of everything else?"

"I've had paramedical training," she said, helping me out of my jacket. "My, ah—my daughter is handicapped."

"The girl in the pictures on the nightstand? She's very pretty."

"Yes she is," she agreed, frowning at the shoulder holster. "My God, if you were wearing that cannon why did you bother to beat up poor Harold? Why didn't you just shoot him a few times?"

"You can't shoot somebody just for trifling with a lady," I said, wincing as I slid out of the Bianchi rig, "it's against the rules. Now if he'd annoyed my horse, or insulted my ranch, you know, something serious . . ."

"Keep it up, Cruz. I'll show you serious."

I unbuttoned my shirt and draped it on the back of the chair. Rachel helped me tug my T-shirt up under my arms.

"Mmmmm," she said, knitting her brow as she examined a welt than ran from the right side of my ribcage to the bruise on my solar plexus. "This does not look good. Hold still."

She ran her fingertips over my skin, lightly tracing each rib all the way around, an exquisitely painful sensation. I clamped my lower lip between my teeth.

"That hurts, doesn't it," she said.

"It hurts and tickles at the same time, and that's one hell of a combination."

"This could be serious. I couldn't feel any obvious breaks, but green-stick fractures don't always show without X-rays. We can wrap this, but you'll have to see a doctor. Can you get your T-shirt off?"

I nodded and tugged it gently over my head. She helped me slide it down my arms. "You, ah, really aren't gonna kick me out in the cold, are you?" I said. "Not after I'm trussed up and helpless."

"Oh, I suppose not," she sighed, unrolling a long strip of gauze, "I mean, how could I explain it to Randolph Scott?"

I awoke around five with an eight-foot lumberjack doing a buck-and-wing on my chest wearing hobnailed boots. Or at least that's what it felt like. Rachel was breathing softly beside me. After she'd finished taping me up, she'd showered and washed her hair and came to bed without makeup, looking scrubbed and shining, wearing a floor-length white flannel nightgown. To prevent any untoward advances, she said. Funny, it seemed to have the opposite effect. The nightgown was lying on her dressing table in a tangled heap, where she'd tossed it at some point during the festivities.

But I was paying some dues for it now. My chest was one giant ache every time I breathed, which was good, because if I'd broken a rib the pain would be sharper and more local-ized. I hoped.

Still, I wasn't going to get much sleep, so I eased carefully out of bed and padded to the bathroom in search of relief.

There were aspirins in the medicine cabinet above the basin, but I was hoping for something stronger, so I checked in the floor-to-ceiling storage cabinet beside the commode. It contained the usual things, spare towels, face cloths, soap, toothpaste. And on a lower shelf, a leather shaving kit.

I ignored it. It was none of my business and I really didn't want to know anyway. But I finished searching the cabinet without turning anything up, sooo . . .

I unzipped the shaving kit, gold-plated safety razor, toothbrush case, fingernail clippers, shaving cream, aftershave, cologne. The same kind of thing I carry in mine, minus the gold plating, of course. Except that I'm partial to Brut, and Mr. Shaving Kit favored English Leather. It seemed to be a popular brand in the area.

I rezipped the kit and put it back, took four aspirins from the medicine cabinet and washed them down with a paper cupful of tap water. I sipped some of the water, trying to rinse away the aftertaste of the aspirin, glancing around the bathroom as I did so.

It was a very nice bathroom. Done in green onyx tile with gold fixtures, a domed, extra-wide tub with a whirlpool. Nothing ostentatious. But very nice. In fact, the whole motel was nice. Neat and clean. And new. Far nicer say, than the restaurant across the street. In fact, it was probably the nicest place in the village by far. A pity.

I crushed the paper cup in my fist and tossed it toward the onyx disposal slot in the wall. I missed, but it didn't matter. The place was too neat anyway.

I padded back out to the living/bedroom and climbed into my jeans with some difficulty, and my socks and Top-Siders. I skipped the T-shirt, and slipped my chamois shirt on very carefully and buttoned it up. Rachel stirred as I dressed, but she didn't awaken.

I stood looking down at her for a moment, and then I sat on the edge of the bed and gently shook her shoulder. Her dark eyes opened immediately, dazed at first, and then startled.

"Bobby?" she said. "What's wrong?"

"Almost everything," I said gently. "I think you'd better tell me about Roland."

Chapter

Seventeen

She sat up slowly, tugging the sheet up to cover her breasts, and brushed her hair back with her fingertips.

"My God, what time is it?" she said.

"Around five. Very early or very late, depending on your point of view."

"I don't owe you an explanation, you know."

"Sure you do. Because he tried to kill me yesterday after you told him I was here."

"What are you talking about?"

"Somebody took a shot at me at the hunting lodge. Several shots, in fact. It had to be Roland or one of his people."

"My God," she said softly.

"Why the surprise? You must have a vague notion of what he's like, what he does for a living."

"I know what he's like," she nodded, "but—when did this happen?"

"Yesterday, noonish, or thereabout."

"No," she said, shaking her head slowly, "I didn't tell them about you until two."

"You talked to him then?"

"Not to Roland," she said with a ghost of a smile, "Mr. Costa doesn't use telephones. One of his people calls every other day or so, always at two, and we give him the registration information, names, addresses, that sort of thing. He didn't call the day you checked in, so—"

"So you're not his only source of information," I said gently, "that doesn't surprise me. He seems to be a very thorough man."

"Yes," she said, "he is."

"Tell me about him."

"I don't think I can do that. You're here to kill him, aren't you, Cruz. You and that—Lugo."

"No. We're here to tell him the war's over. Nothing more, I swear."

"It doesn't matter," she said, "I couldn't help you if I wanted to. I don't know where he is. And I can't very well pass him a message without admitting that I've . . . talked to you about him. And I don't want to do that. He's been very good to me, but he's—he can be very hard, do you understand?"

"I understand that you might feel loyalty for him, or more, but if I don't find him soon, he'll probably try to take me out again and one of us might get killed this time. And for nothing. Do you want that?"

"That's a stupid question. You know I don't want anything like that."

"Then help me," I said simply.

"I don't know," she said doubtfully, "I don't know if I can. What do you want to know?"

"Everything. Anything. Tell me about him."

"There's not that much to tell. When my daughter was born, my husband—left us. I was broke and alone in Detroit with a baby, I didn't know a soul. So I called Mr. Costa. I'd known who he was since I was a girl, you know, to say hello to. And he offered to help me."

"Out of the kindness of his heart."

"You know, a little self-righteousness can go a long way at five in the morning," she said coolly. "Of course it wasn't out of the kindness of his heart. But I had a handicapped daughter to consider, who needed special care. Expensive care. It wasn't a difficult choice. Roland can be a very charming man, and I was very grateful."

"Yes, I suppose so."

"If you didn't want to know, you shouldn't have asked."

"I wish it was that simple," I said. "Does he come here often?"

"No, and when his wife is along, they stay at the beach house, or the lodge. And he—visits—"

"And when she's not, he stays here. But doesn't register?"

"That's right."

"Have you—seen him recently, or talked to him?"

"No, but we only get the calls when he and Rol Junior are in the area, and we've been getting them for several weeks now."

"Do you have any way of contacting him?"

"No. Only by calling his offices in Detroit. And then only in an emergency."

"And you have no idea where he might be? Anyone he might stay with?"

"No, I'm afraid not. I never met his . . . friends, you know. We didn't socialize."

"Lucky you," I said. "I've met some of his friends. You wouldn't like them. This may sound odd, but does the name Tigger mean anything to you? Or Leo the Lion?"

"Aside from children's stories, not a thing. Anything else?"

"No," I said, releasing a long, ragged breath, "nothing I can think of."

"Then I think you'd better go. And I don't think we should see each other again."

"I don't agree. I want to see you again. Very much."

"What you want doesn't matter very much, Cruz, or what I want either. Shannon's care costs twenty-eight thousand dollars a year. Are you a rich man, Cruz? Can you help me out with that?"

I didn't say anything, which was an answer of sorts.

"I didn't think so," she said. "Then do you mind? I have a long day tomorrow, or today. Or whatever it is."

"Do you really have to work so hard," I said, "considering your—arrangement?"

"That's really none of your business, is it?" she said.

"No, I guess not. Sorry."

"So am I," she said. "I'm sorry I didn't meet you that summer. Instead of Arnie."

"I think I am too," I said. I got up and collected my gun and windbreaker. " 'Bye, Rachel. I hope things work out for you."

She didn't hear me. She was staring off into space, frowning. "Leo Taggart?" she said suddenly.

"What?"

"Leo the Lion? Tigger. Could that be Leo Taggart?"

"I don't know, who's Leo Taggart?"

"I don't really know him, I only met him once, at the restaurant."

"With Roland?"

"No he was with friends, but Roland might know him. He owns a hunting lodge in the Ojibwas near Roland's. Ten thousand acres, I think. The Big Bear? Does that sound right?"

"Maybe. Do you remember what he looks like?"

"I really don't. It was several years ago, and I meet a lot of people in my business."

"Yes," I said, "I suppose you do."

★ ★ ★ ★ ★

Someone was knocking on the door of the beach house. I was in the kitchen, rooting through the debris with fungus crawling up my arms. And then the knocking came again and I knew it was Roland and he had a branding iron and I didn't want him to catch me but I was tangled in the fungus and . . . I gradually surfaced. I was lying on the bed in my room, fully dressed except for my shoes with my windbreaker over me.

And someone was pounding on the door.

I glanced at the travel alarm. Ten after eight. Rachel? I'd fallen asleep with the Beretta for company. I slipped it out of its holster and padded to the window.

An Algoma County cruiser was parked in front of my cabin, idling. Terrific. I set the chain lock and eased the door open a crack.

"Get your coat," Clinton Mattis said, "the sheriff wants you to come look at a body."

Chapter

Eighteen

"What's this all about?" I said, "Where are we going?"

We were headed north out of the village in Mattis's patrol car. My side felt like one giant bruise and my head felt worse.

"We're goin' to the cemetery," Mattis growled, "that's where they keep the bodies, ain't it?"

"Whose body?"

"You tell me. Way I understand it this is your party. All I know is, I got off patrol at four this morning and Ira calls me at seven, says to go round up Hec Michaud and Paulie Croft 'cause them state cops showed up with an exhumation order for Charlie Costa. And he said after I rousted Hec and Paulie I should pick you up. State cops said you gave 'em the idea and if we gotta be out at the goddamn cemetery at this goddamn hour of the goddamn morning, then you can goddamn well be out there too."

"Oh," I said.

Mattis wheeled into the church parking lot with an angry spray of gravel and slid to a halt beside a midnight blue state police cruiser. I climbed out and he slammed the car into reverse and roared off, fishtailing down the highway.

The entertainment up on the hill was well underway. LeClair and the two State troopers were grouped around the open grave. Paulie was sitting on the tailgate of a flatbed truck with a winch and boom rig mounted on the rear. Hec Michaud was chest deep in the grave, shoveling furiously.

A bitter northerly wind tugged at my clothing as I trudged up the gravel path, and snowflakes drifted down out of the gunmetal gray sky.

"Cruz," Sheriff LeClair nodded curtly, "Lieutenant Schmitke here tells me we have you to thank for this little party."

"Paulie told me the coffin jammed when they tried to lower it because it was too heavy. I just passed it along."

"Well if you'd passed it along to me, I could've told you the equipment out here's all World War I surplus, like everything else in this county."

Schmitke glanced up at us but didn't say anything. I wandered over to the flatbed truck to say hello to Paulie. He was sitting with his long legs dangling over the tailgate, wearing faded denim work clothes, a white dressing on the back of his head, and a gloomy expression.

"Hello, Paulie," I said, "look, I want to thank you for jumping in last night, I—"

"I shouldna done it," he said, frowning, "I got hurt and now Hec's doin' my job. I don't wanna lose my job, Flower."

"Hec doesn't look like he's having much fun. Don't worry, he'll have you working again as soon as you're able. Maybe sooner."

"C'mon Paulie," Hec shouted, "get the damn cable down here and let's get this sonofabitch up!"

"See what I mean," I said, but Paulie was already scrambling up to release the winch. He slowly unwound the end of the steel cable down into the pit. Hec hooked it to a ring embedded in the concrete vault lid, and climbed out.

Paulie jerked the winch lever down and the motor

hummed to life, drawing the cable taut, and slowly lifting the concrete slab up out of the grave. When it was clear, Michaud and the two State troopers pushed it to one side and Paulie released the cable, dropping it to the ground.

"You want the box hauled up or ya gonna open it down there?" Hec asked, glaring at me.

"I think we can take a look without raising the casket," Schmitke said. "If we find anything we can haul it up."

"Well you're gonna have to open it your own selves," Hec said flatly, "I'm the sexton here. I ain't no fuckin' grave robber. This ain't my job."

"I'm wearing a clean uniform," Schmitke said.

"Me too," Yaeger echoed. Everyone was staring at me.

"Hey," I said, "I'm not going down there."

"This was your idea," Yaeger said, "seems to me you oughta be elected. What's the matter, Cruz, you superstitious?"

"No," I said, feeling a surge of anger, "and I'm not afraid of smudging my cute little outfit either."

I stalked to the head of the grave and lowered myself carefully into the pit. The coffin was resting in a concrete vault with walls about three inches thick. I straddled it, keeping my feet on the cement. It seemed warmer down in the grave out of the wind, or possibly because I was six feet closer to hell.

"The lid release lugs are on the right side," LeClair offered helpfully.

"I know where they are," I snapped. I'm not particularly superstitious, but I'll admit I wasn't too happy about blundering around in an open grave. Especially when somebody was already using it. I knelt on the coffin and reached down into the dark between the coffin and the vault, groping for the lug release, willing myself not to think about anything.

I found the handle and jerked it. The front quarter of the

coffin popped up a few inches with a *whuff* of fetid air, sour and foul. I'm sure my imagination made it worse than it was, but it was bad enough. I swallowed rapidly a few times, took a deep breath, and then opened the lid.

The coffin lid was upholstered with deeply tufted white silk. A coverlet of the same material was over the body and I tugged it back. Charles Costa's head was resting on a large, white silk pillow, but not peacefully. His face was distorted, his mouth and right eye partially open. A dark puddle of nameless goo had congealed on the pillow beside his left ear.

"Sweet Jesus," someone murmured softly, and I realized it was me.

"Any, ah," Schmitke cleared his throat, "any room for another body in there?"

"I'm not sure," I said, "have you got a ruler, something I can measure with?"

LeClair passed me an ordinary wooden yardstick. I measured the distance from the bed of the casket to the rim, and from the outer rim to the base of the coffin, trying to ignore Charlie Costa's milky, unwavering stare. Twenty inches deep inside, roughly twenty-five inches outside.

"No way," I said, "he's all by himself."

"Shit," Yaeger muttered.

"I knew it was for fuckin' nothin'," Hec said viciously, "Nothin'! Whole damn thing's just a waste of time!"

"Well, at least we know one more place she isn't," I said.

"You might as well check the rest of it," Schmitke sighed, "just in case."

I nodded and released the other two lugs, leaning back out of the way as I raised the lid. I tugged the coverlet off. Charlie'd gone first cabin. He was wearing an eight-hundred-dollar black silk suit, a Sulka tie, and patent leather Florsheim boots. A film of gray-green mildew was spreading

169

Doug Allyn

upward from around his groin toward his face.

"Shit," Yaeger said again.

I tossed the coverlet back over the body and closed both lids. When I'd resecured the lugs—LeClair offered me a hand up out of the grave, which surprised me. I'd half-expected him to start filling it in with me in it. Schmitke and Yaeger were already halfway down the hill, headed for their cruiser.

"Win a few, lose a few," LeClair said.

"I wouldn't know," I said, "I haven't won any lately."

"Cruz oughta be the one fills in the goddamn hole," Hec said, "this's his mess."

"When Mr. Cruz starts drawing county money for working out here he can fill in graves," LeClair said mildly, "meantime, you take care of it, Hec. You. Not Paulie."

"The Mex'll prob'ly wanna lend a hand anyway," Michaud sneered, "diggin's usually wetback work."

LeClair grabbed my arm before I could move. Hec backed away, brandishing his shovel. "C'mon, Greaser, you want some a this?"

"Let it go, Cruz," LeClair said quietly. "If you two kill each other I'll have to bury you both myself, and I ain't got the energy. Come on, I'll give you a lift back to town."

"Sorry about Hec," LeClair said, as we drove slowly back to town in his patrol car. "He's a jerk, but my daddy told me if you try to whup all the jerks you meet in this life, your hands are gonna be too sore to get any work done."

"Your daddy was probably right," I said, smiling reluctantly, "but one of these days Hec's mouth's going to get him in serious trouble. Maybe with me."

"Way I hear it about half the folks in Tubby's had serious problems with you last night. And Paulie needed eight stitches in the back of his head because of it."

170

"I'm sorry about that. Things . . . got out of hand. It won't happen again."

"Good," he said, "glad to hear it."

"You don't seem angry about this fiasco this morning."

"Oh I wasn't too pleased about bein' rousted out, but there wasn't any major harm done, except maybe to Clint's beauty sleep. And I got a little somethin' to needle Schmitke with out of it. Can't say Charlie looked too happy about bein' disturbed though, did he?"

"No, he didn't. Funny about that."

"About what?"

"His features being distorted like that. Usually when a victim sustains a head injury, they bring his features back to normal by injecting a fixative, a sort of liquid plastic. Once that stuff hardens I wouldn't think you could change his expression with a baseball bat."

"So?"

"So nothing," I said. "I'm not saying it means anything. For all I know he's just been laying down there contemplating his sins."

"I don't think so," LeClair said, chuckling softly, "he didn't look anywhere near sorry enough to me."

"No," I said, "maybe not."

Chapter

Nineteen

I stood in front of my cabin for a moment, watching LeClair's patrol car swing back out on the highway, then I unlocked my door and hurried in. I shucked my Top-Siders and put on heavy wool socks and hiking boots, took the Bianchi shoulder rig off the peg in the closet and strapped it on and put my windbreaker on over it. I grabbed the blaze-orange vest and opened the door. And Enrique Lugo was standing there.

"You're fired," he said.

"I'm what?"

"You're fired," he repeated, pushing me back into the room by jabbing his forefinger into my chest.

"Hey, easy," I said, "what's the matter with you?"

"You think I'm some kinda clown? You make wisecracks, you think I don't get 'em? I get 'em. But I let 'em pass because they ain't important. Because you ain't important. Well that's over."

"Look, I don't know what's eating you, but—"

"You are, Cruz. You're hired to do a job but then you say you won't do this or that. And then instead of takin' care of the punk-ass business you're supposed to, you're out playin' footsie with these hicktown cops diggin' up Charlie's grave. His fuckin' *grave!* You're supposed to be lookin' for Roland and Rollie. We already know where Charlie is, man. The same place you're gonna be when Eladio hears about this!" He jabbed at my chest again but I snatched his forefinger in my fist, bending it back slightly.

"Relax, Enrique," I said, "she wasn't there."

He stared into my face, reading me. "Let go of my finger."

"You gonna stop poking me in the chest? It hurts."

He nodded and I let him go. "What are you talking about? Who's not there?"

"The girl," I said, "Cindy Stanek. You don't give a damn about Charlie's grave, you're just afraid you'll be in a jam with your people if I help the police find the girl. Well, I tried, but we didn't find her. She wasn't there. But she was supposed to be. Wasn't she?"

"I don't know what you mean."

"I guess it doesn't matter. Since I'm fired."

"I don't know if you're fired," he said, scowling, "I got to think."

"Don't think."

"What do you mean, don't—"

"Look, you did me a favor last night, now I'll do you one. Wait. Don't do anything. I may have a line on Roland. It shouldn't take long to check out. Give me a day. If you tell Bradleigh the girl's missing again he'll send an army up here."

"Maybe," Lugo conceded, "but if he finds out from some-body else that you're helpin' the cops, he might have us both whacked and sort it out later."

"At least wait until tonight, then. Look, we want to turn up the Costas, right? It's what we're here for. Well, maybe I can if you just give me a few hours."

"I don't think so," he said slowly, "I think you're jackin' me around."

"After you saved my neck?"

"Look, I didn't do you no favors, Cruz. I just figured if them paddies stomped you through the floor I'd be stuck in this toilet till you got outa the hospital is all. So nobody owes nobody nothin'. And I got a bad feelin' about this. Thing is, if it goes wrong, I could get killed, you know? We both could. I think maybe I'll go with you this time."

"No way," I said, shaking my head.

"You don't think I can keep up my end?"

"It's not that. Hell, you're terrific in restaurants, and probably back alleys, but if I have to go into the hills after these guys—Do you have boots? Hunting clothes? No? I didn't think so."

"You give me your word?" he said abruptly.

"What?"

"You want me to hold off callin' Bradleigh? Then gimme your word you'll do the right thing, you won't fuck me up. Gimme your word."

"You must be kidding. What do I do, swear on a Bible?"

"No," he said seriously, "you gimme your word, man to man, that's all."

"Fine," I said, "I give you my word."

"Okay," he nodded, "you go do what you gotta, I'll see you later." He paused in the doorway. "Hey, man," he said with an odd smile, "you think you're lyin' to me, but you ain't. You're *Raza,* whether you know it or not. Blood in, blood out, Cruz. *Adios.*"

"Ad— I'll see you around," I said.

I put the vest on over my jacket after he'd gone. He was dead wrong, of course. If the girl was with the Costas, I'd dump the whole thing in Schmitke's lap and Lugo would have to look out for himself. He'd kill her, and I wouldn't be a party to that, word or no word. So I'd lied to him. In a good cause. He was scum anyway, an ex-con who killed people for money. Scum. Still, I wish I hadn't given him my word. I don't know why. But I wish I hadn't.

I remembered passing a sign that said Big Bear Lodge on my way to the Costa's lodge, so I pointed the Ford north into the Ojibwas. As I drove past the turnoff to the cemetery I glimpsed Hec and Paulie winching the vault cover back into place. It was a bitter day for working with cold steel cable and concrete. The sky was leaden and the snow was falling steadily now, fat wet flakes plummeting straight down, too heavy to be blown about by the wind, blanketing the country-side. Instant winter. By the time I'd driven up into the hills I could only see a few car lengths ahead, and the road signs were nearly invisible.

But I managed to find it. Sort of. The Big Bear sign wasn't for the lodge itself, only for the county road that led back to it. I kept the Mustang at a crawl because of the snow and to keep from bouncing my ribs around, but I wasn't worried about missing the lodge. The land on both sides of the road was marked with steel posts, one every twenty feet, each with a bright yellow aluminum sign, BIG BEAR KEEP OUT. A single strand of wire ran between the posts, to meet the legal requirements for trespass, a fence meant for people, not animals.

The gate was much larger than the Costas', towering over a three-lane drive. It was fashioned out of peeled logs, to give it a rustic look. The sign overhead was a massive slab of unfinished wood with BIG BEAR burned into it. Interesting. I wondered if Taggart had done that part himself.

The broad drive meandered through an open, park-like forest for most of a mile. Several smaller roads forked away from it, and I was wondering if perhaps one of them led to the lodge when I topped a low rise and there it was. And well worth the wait.

175

The Big Bear looked like a prop fortress from "Drums Along the Mohawk." It was a huge log cabin, half a block long and two stories high. A front porch topped by a widow's walk stretched the width of the building, made of gigantic oak logs still wearing their bark. The only things missing were brass cannons on the parapets and Iron Eyes Cody skulking around in buckskin underwear.

The frontier outpost effect was marred a bit by the dozen-odd cars parked in a long lean-to beside the building, all late model, *creme-de-la-creme*, Benzes, Caddies, BMWs. There was no silver Lincoln limo, but then I hadn't expected to see it right out front. I parked my lowly Ford next to the hitching rail in front of the porch, wishing I had a hank of clothesline to tether it so it wouldn't wander off somewhere to graze.

A wrist-thick length of knotted hemp was hanging beside the ornately carved double doors, with a sign above it that said Bell. I tugged it, half-expecting a war whoop, and I wasn't far wrong. An Indian woman answered the door, tall, cocoa-eyed, and handsome, her dark hair cut short and tightly curled. But no buckskins. She was wearing a bright pink blouse and sprayed-on designer jeans.

"Yes?"

"Hi, my name's Cruz. Would you tell Mr. Taggart a friend of Roland Costa's would like to see him, and tell him it's urgent."

She eyed me a moment, trying to decide how urgent it could be, then shrugged. "Come on in," she said, "I'll see if he's here."

I followed her in. The heavy door closed behind me automatically with a gentle *shush*. Boonesboro was never like this.

The room was the size of a basketball court, lit by wagon-wheel chandeliers dangling from anchor chains salvaged from the Andrea Doria. It was furnished with overstuffed leather armchairs and sofas, a Cinerama-sized TV screen in one corner and a fieldstone fireplace large enough to burn whole trees in the other. A series of trophy heads stared blindly down from their mounts near the ceiling, elk, bear, antelope, even a tiger. A glory hunter's dream, a conservationist's nightmare. The air was thick with cigar smoke and conversation from a poker game at a banquet table at the far end of the room. A half-dozen men were clustered around it, clad in various mixtures of hunting garb and long underwear.

I waited in the center of the room while the Indian woman spoke to the man seated at the head of the table. He eyed me a moment, then nodded and tossed in his hand. A few of the others checked me out with mild curiosity, but resumed the game as Taggart walked over.

He was a heavily built, barrel of a man, square-faced, sleek, and prosperous, five-ten, with dark brown hair, silvering at the temples. Kenny was right. A very classy guy. He was dressed casually, a blaze-orange flannel shirt and khaki slacks, but they fit as though they'd been tailored for him, and I guessed that they had been. His beer stein was made of beaten silver and monogrammed.

"Mr. Cruz, is it?" he said, frowning, "I'm Leo Taggart. I, ah, know a few of Roland's friends, but I don't believe we've met." He offered me a grizzly-sized paw. If his handshake was a test of strength, I lost.

"We haven't," I said, "I'm a business associate of Mr. Costa's. From Detroit."

"I see. Sacheen said the matter was urgent?"

"Life and death, you might say. I want you to get a message to Roland for me."

"A message?" he said, raising his eyebrows, "I'm afraid there's been some sort of mix-up. I haven't seen Roland since mid-summer, fourth of July weekend, I believe. He sometimes drops by for a visit during the season, but if the matter's urgent then I suggest you contact him at his own lodge. It's—"

"I know where it is. He's not there. But he told me that if I ever needed to contact him in an emergency, I should see you."

"Really. How odd. I've known Roland for years, of course, we're neighbors. But as I said, I haven't seen him in months."

"But you've seen Rollie," I said.

"Rollie?" he coughed, "why, ah, yes, I saw him oh, sometime in September, I believe. Forgive me, I'm being a terrible host. Sacheen! Bring Mr. Cruz an ale! A man needs a little fortification in this weather, eh? Do you, ah, hunt, Mr. Cruz?"

"Not animals. Not anymore."

"I've taken game all over the world, Africa, India. The hunting's played out there now, but there are still some challenges left. For instance, did you notice the two whitetail trophies over the fireplace? Both mine, both Boone and Crockett entries."

"Very impressive," I said, nodding my thanks to the Indian woman for the iced mug of ale. "What did you take them with?"

"A Ferlach double in 270 Winchester. Some might consider it a bit light, but I prefer the challenge, and it doesn't damage the hides as much as the larger calibers."

"Like say, a 30/06 might?"

"Exactly. It's a popular caliber, but it's really a bit much for deer."

"It seems to work pretty well on houses," I said.

"Houses?" he frowned. "Oh, you mean in military applications. Yes, it's a popular military caliber, or was, actually."

"Do you own any 30/06's?"

"I believe I have several in my collection. A Browning

Safari grade and . . . one or two others. I can't recall off-hand."

"Do you have any military surplus steel-jacketed ammo in this little collection of yours?"

"No. I only have sporting weapons. Why do you ask?"

"Just curious. Look Leo, I can understand why you're reluctant to accept me at face value. Rollie said you might be. And he told me to use the password."

"Password?"

"Right. Pooh Bear. Tigger. Leo the Lion."

He paled and flinched as though I'd struck him. He glanced hurriedly over at the card players, then back to me. "What the hell do you want?" he said hoarsely.

"Just what I said. I want you to give them a message. Tell them Lugo wants to talk. We'll be waiting at the motel. And tell them to keep the girl healthy in the meantime."

"But I can't tell them anything," he said desperately, "I swear to you, I don't know where they are."

"Sure you do, Pooh Bear, you know exactly where they are. They're in Christopher Robin's little hideaway, or whatever you call it. So don't waltz me around, just give them the message. And remember the part about keeping the girl healthy. Or would you like me to make a little announcement to your friends right now. Tigger."

"All right, all right, for God's sake keep your voice down. I'll try to give them your message. That's all I can do."

"Your best had better be good enough, Leo, or I'll be back to look for them with a brass band. And we'll be very noisy. About all of it. Understand?"

He nodded mutely.

"Good. Nice place you've got here," I said, glancing around, "but it smells a little ripe. Maybe it's all those dead animals on your walls. Why'd you shoot so many, Leo?

Trying to prove a little something, are we?"

"Get out," he said tautly.

"Sure," I said, "but remember the message. Oops! Darn, I dropped my glass. So sorry. Clumsy of me, wasn't it. But then that's me. Clumsy. And noisy. You remember that, Tigger. I'll see you around."

Chapter

Twenty

I drove the Mustang out of sight of the lodge, then turned down the first fork I came to and pulled off the drive. Grabbing the mini-binoculars out of the glove compartment, I jogged back up the track. I found a sheltered spot in a stand of cedars roughly sixty yards from the lodge with a view of the porch and carport. Easing down with my back against the bole of a large cedar, I began glassing the fortress and the grounds through the steadily falling snow.

I didn't have to wait long. Taggart came out the front door wearing a camouflage hunting suit, carrying a rifle. He paused long enough to give some last minute instructions to the Indian woman, then stalked off around the building. She stared after him for a moment, then closed the door, leaving me with a view of precisely nothing.

Cursing silently, I gave up my shelter and began circling to my left, trying to see where he'd gone. He'd disappeared. I scanned the lodge and the carport, even the trees on the far side of the clearing. Nothing.

There was a shed at the end of the carport, but it was much too small to be— The door of the shed swung open, spilling a golden pool of light onto the snow, and Taggart roared out of it mounted on a snowmobile, revving its engine, its single headlight glaring at the afternoon like a cyclops. He turned the machine toward the forest, gunned it, and was off, disappearing into the trees in a matter of seconds.

And I was off too, pounding up the drive after him, slipping and skidding in the snow, realizing I had no chance before I'd run ten yards. He could cover more ground in a half-hour than I could in a day. Unless—

I charged past the carport through the open door of the shed. There were two more snowmobiles, top-of-the-line Ski-doo Safari Grands, sleek as torpedoes and twice as expensive. The Big Bear was a class establishment. And a trusting one. The keys were in them.

I cautiously straddled the machine nearest the door.

The controls hadn't changed much, though it'd been a long time since I'd ridden one. Speedometer, tachometer, fuel and temp, gauges. And ignition. I flicked the key and the motor thrummed to life. The fuel gauge came up to Full, and everything else seemed normal. What the hell. I tweaked the thumb throttle on the handlebars and the machine eased into motion like a Rolls Royce gliding downhill.

I swung it to the left as soon as I was clear of the door, following Taggart's track into the trees. I kept the speed down around fifteen miles per hour. I wasn't dressed for serious snowmobiling, no goggles or helmet, or even gloves, and I didn't want to risk frostbite trying to keep up with him.

I was able to follow his track without using the headlight, but just barely. The wet snow was stinging my face and running into my eyes, and my hands quickly numbed on the grips. The damned trail seemed to go on forever, looping and twisting through the forest. And then it began to climb.

We were in the foothills of the Ojibwa Mountains now, gently rolling slopes, sparsely timbered with aspen and pine, open, empty country, unfarmable, but good territory for deer and elk. And at one time, wolves. The track slanted gradually upward along the eastern bank of a narrow ridge, leveling out as it neared the crest. And then it stopped.

Taggart's machine was parked in a grove of silver birch, with a few cedar boughs tossed over it for concealment. He was nowhere in sight. The ridge ended twenty or thirty yards ahead, and there was a broad valley beyond, but no sign of a cabin or anything resembling one. I shut down the Ski-doo, my ears ringing in the sudden silence.

"Get off the machine," Taggart said quietly, "and step away from it. Keep your hands where I can see them."

He was somewhere in the grove of birches ahead of me. I couldn't see him, but it didn't matter. He could see me, and he had a rifle. No contest. I climbed off the Ski-doo, rubbing my palms together to get the circulation going.

"Walk toward me, into the trees."

I spotted him then, standing beside a large birch. I could also see the rifle. I was looking down its bore. A 270 seems much larger from that angle. I stopped when we were about ten yards apart.

"You said you'd wait at the motel," he said accusingly.

"Yeah, well, I lied. I apologize. Shall we get on with it?"

"Get on with what?"

"I have a message. Just let me deliver it and we can all go home."

"I'm afraid it's not that simple," he said.

"No?" I thought it might not be. "So what've you got in mind?"

"I'm not sure. I'm a little out of my depth here."

"Then take me to Roland."

"I ah, don't suppose you'd believe me if I told you they weren't here."

"Not a chance. They shot at me yesterday, and as soon as I lit a candle under you, you made a beeline for the backwoods.

Look, the game's over. Take me to them."

"All right," he nodded, "I suppose it doesn't matter. You already know about this place."

"What place?"

"The Den," he said, surprised, "you're standing on it."

A slanted trapdoor was neatly hidden in the grove of birches. Taggart had been standing by it when I drove up. I moved ahead of him down a short flight of concrete steps to an ordinary brown windowless steel door. I stopped, with his rifle barrel pressing against my spine. He tapped me on the shoulder and held out a key in his left hand.

"Unlock it, then knock, three long, and two short. Twice."

I did as he instructed, first the key, then the knocks, all the while picturing the empty automatic weapons slots in the gun safe at the lodge. And Kenny's brand.

I turned the knob and swung the metal door inward. I felt a rush of cool air, but I couldn't see anything. The room was in total darkness.

"Roland, Rollie, don't shoot!" Taggart shouted, "I'm coming in. The light switch is on your left," he added.

I fumbled around the doorjamb, found the switch, and we stepped into the room.

It was much as Kenny described it, open and without windows, its walls paneled with rough cedar. There were bunk beds and a single bed against the near wall, an efficiency kitchen in the far corner, a rifle rack with a half-dozen paramilitary automatic weapons in it. Three comfortable-looking easy chairs faced a television/stereo console. There were a few magazines in a rack between the easy chairs, but there were no books in sight. And nobody.

"Where are they?" I said.

"Roland! Rollie?" Taggart called, his voice very loud in

the silent room. Then he chuckled. "I guess they must have stepped out."

"You sonofabitch!" I said, turning to face him. "They're not here."

"That's right. I told you that."

"Then where are they?"

"I have no idea. I haven't seen either of them since September, nor had any contact from them."

"But they're up here somewhere. Somebody shot at me yesterday at the lodge."

"With a 30/06 you mean? Is that what all the questions were about?"

"That's right. You, maybe, Leo?"

"Where did the shots come from?"

"From the trees across the meadow. I was standing on the deck."

"What is that, sixty or seventy yards? You've seen my trophies. I assure you I couldn't have missed you from that distance, nor would Rollie. He's an excellent shot. Roland can't fire a rifle at all, arthritic shoulder. I have no idea who it could have been."

"Whoever it was used military ammo, steel-jacketed bullets."

"I believe Rollie has some for a few of the guns in his collection," Taggart shrugged, "but that doesn't mean anything. Military surplus ammunition is quite common. You can buy it almost anywhere."

"What was the bit with the knocking just now?"

"Just my little joke," he said coolly, "you were very pushy in front of my friends. Very pushy." He gestured with the rifle. "Walk over to the single bed and sit down."

Our gazes met and held. "No," I said, "I don't think so."

His grip tightened on the rifle. "I said move."

"No. It's over, Leo. Roland built this place to use in an emergency. Well, he had one. It got Charlie killed. If he ever intended to use it, they'd be here. They're not coming."

"But I still can't let you—"

"Listen to me," I interrupted, "these people, Roland's people, are like an army. And if I disappear out here, they'll think he's here and they'll be on you like a pack of wolves. And they'll feed you your fingers a joint at a time until you tell them where he is. And you won't be able to, will you? Because you don't know."

"No," he said, "I don't. I don't understand why they didn't come here if they were in trouble."

"They're not the only ones missing. Charlie's lady friend has dropped out of sight too. Cindy Stanek?"

"The overly mammaried Cindy," he nodded, "that might explain it. She never liked it up here, not even the beach house. A city girl, born and bred. And bred and bred."

"You think she and Roland—"

"He's always been very much the ladies' man. Especially other people's ladies. I think he likes the danger. The perversity of taking his brother's woman might appeal to him, but she's not really his type. He usually prefers them younger and less . . . shopworn."

"Yes," I sighed, "so I understand."

"We worked very hard to build this place," he said absently, glancing around the room, "the three of us. We flew in some Canadian workmen from Vancouver to do the heavy work, but we finished the rest of it ourselves, Roland, Rollie and me. It was a . . . very special summer, in a way. Rollie was sixteen then, just reaching his manhood. God, he was beautiful. Since then this has been our special place, he—"

"Leo," I said, "if you say one more word I'm going to vomit. Right here in your special place."

"You're a cold insensitive bastard."

"I know. That's what my ex-wife said, too."

"I'm not surprised," he snapped, but the gun barrel wavered a little. Not much, but a little, and I began to think I might survive.

"Shall we, ah—go now?" I said.

"You go," he said, lowering the rifle, "I think I'd like to be alone here for awhile."

"Sure. I understand."

"I doubt that," he sighed, "I doubt it very much."

Chapter

Twenty-One

The ride back to the lodge seemed much longer and colder than the trip out. Another time, it could have been pure pleasure, humming through the snow-covered hills on a finely tuned machine, but I was chilled and wet, and my ribs hurt. And even my anger couldn't warm me.

Lugo was right after all. We were on a wild goose chase. The Costas were working on their tans down in the Caymans while we blundered around the backwoods like winos at an art auction.

I left the Ski-doo in the shed and hiked through the snow to the Mustang. I fired it up, but I didn't drive off immediately. I sat there awhile instead, letting the heater thaw my frozen carcass, and tried to work through the situation.

But in the end, it just wouldn't compute. I kept coming back to the shooting. If it wasn't the Costas, or one of their people . . .

I played that morning back in my mind, the run with Rachel, LeClair's office, back to the motel, then the cemetery. Then the trashed lodge, the deck, the gunfire, the steady *whump* of the bullets blowing through the walls.

Steel-jacketed bullets. Paramilitary? Or just army surplus. The firing was slow and steady, and not very accurate. Taggart was right, the sniper hadn't missed me by much, but he shouldn't have missed me at all. I wouldn't have missed me at that distance.

So he was a bad shot. Or his gun was inaccurate. An old gun? An old army surplus weapon shooting surplus ammo, not because the sniper was a paramilitary freak, but just because the stuff was cheap? Possibly. Only why shoot at me at all? Because I'm not terrific at social interaction? Or because I was a threat to someone?

I slipped the Ford into gear and drove thoughtfully back toward town.

When I passed the turn-off to the cemetery, I pulled off on the shoulder a moment, and glassed the area with my binoculars. The flatbed truck with the winch was still parked near Charlie's grave, but the site was deserted, and the snow was already erasing the evidence of the desecration. But it didn't cover everything. In fact, it made some things much easier to see.

I put the binoculars back in the glove compartment, and drove on into Algoma.

The village was bustling, filled with Saturday afternoon shoppers and strolling red-suits who'd called it a day because of the snow. I had to park in the central lot off the main street and walk back, but I had no trouble finding the place I was looking for. I'd been passing it for days without really paying any attention to it, a narrow storefront office with Village of Algoma stenciled crudely on a plywood sign in the window.

The clerk literally dragged himself to the counter, a stroke-shattered old hulk of a man with a paralyzed leg, his left arm strapped to his belt, and the side of his weather-beaten face sagging like so much melted wax. His cheek was distorted even further by a huge cud of tobacco. He leaned his good arm on the counter and spat a stream of brown juice in the general direction of the spittoon in the corner. Dead center. Two points.

"Do somethin' for ya?" he asked.

"I hope so. I'd like to see a plat book for the county, please."

"Plat book? Sure, got one right here." He pulled a slim folder from beneath the counter and flipped it open to Ojibwa County. "Some of these titles ain't current, but I know most of the landholders around here. Any particular parcel in mind?"

I traced the line of the main road north with my fingertip to where it forked off. "Here, the land around the cemetery."

"Well, there's houses north and south of it, but—"

"No, not the houses. I'm interested in these fields around it to the west. All of that property seems to be owned by— somebody named Lund?"

"Mike Lund," he nodded. "He don't live in Algoma no more. Moved south like everybody else. But he still owns the land."

"It has corn growing on it now."

"I believe he's farming it on shares with Hec Michaud. Hec put in some raggedy-ass corn this spring. Never did come in good enough to be worth harvestin' so he just left it stand. Hec ain't much of a farmer."

"I thought he was in charge of the cemetery?"

"He is. You from the city?"

I nodded.

"Figured so," he said, and spat another stream toward the spittoon. "See, in a place like Algoma, a man can't make it with just one job. Most folks do a little of this and that to get by. I clerk here and got my social insecurity. Hec does the cemetery, paints houses sometimes, and does a little farmin' now and again."

"How about the sheriff," I asked, "he do a little farming too?"

"Sometimes," he said, examining me carefully with his good eye, "sometimes he does."

LeClair was alone in the Sheriff's Office, leaning back in his chair with his muddy Wellingtons up on his desk, snoring softly. I let the door slam behind me and he jerked awake.

"What the hell—? Oh, it's you," he said groggily, massaging his eyelids with his fingertips. "What time is it?"

"A little after three," I said, wandering to the coffee urn in the corner, "you want a cup?"

"I wouldn't mind. I had kind of an early morning."

"So I heard," I said, filling two Styrofoam cups. I handed one to LeClair and sat on the edge of his desk. "Where is everybody?"

"Lavina goes home at noon on Saturdays." He winced at the bitter taste of the coffee. "Clint doesn't come on until five."

"Good, I, ah, I'd like to talk to you about something."

"God, who do you want to dig up now?"

"Nothing like that. This is more along the lines of—an opportunity. You know who the people I'm working for are?"

"I guess so," he said guardedly, "why?"

"They're, ah, interested in making some investments in your area, nothing heavy, but it might require your—cooperation, in a small way. Say an occasional wink. And it could be a very profitable wink. Very, very profitable."

"I see." He took a sip of his coffee. "A wink."

"That's right."

He didn't say anything for a moment, but a flush slowly crept above his collar. "Cruz," he said tightly, "I noticed you gave Paulie your 'Nam bracelet yesterday at the hill. That was

191

a nice thing to do. So because of that, and because you're a city boy and don't know any better, I'm gonna give you thirty seconds to get out of my office, and fifteen minutes to get the hell out of my town. How's that for a wink, Mister?"

"Not bad," I said, "take a wink at this." I tossed the joint Paulie'd given me on the desk.

"What is it?"

"What's it look like? Open it up. Take a look at the weed."

Still scowling, he tore the paper apart, spilling the filler on the desk. He picked up a bud, squeezed it between his fingers, and sniffed it. "This is green and it hasn't been laced. I'd guess it local, right? Where did you get it?"

"It was a gift from a guy who knows how to live off the land. As an informant, he'll have to remain anonymous, of course."

"Gee," he said dryly, "I wonder who it could be? Where did your informant get it?"

"In the cornfields near the cemetery. There's an area to the southwest where every fourth or fifth plant is marijuana."

"Hec Michaud!" he said, slamming his fist on the desktop. "I knew it! I knew something was wrong out there, he was way too pushy, but I thought it was—just you, maybe. How much is out there?"

"It's not the French Connection, twenty or thirty plants, and they've already been harvested, but there's enough left for a righteous bust on it."

"A bust," he said acidly, "not a wink?"

"No, not a wink. To, ah, to tell you the truth I thought you might already be winking. I'm sorry about that, but like you said, I'm from out of town."

He stared at me for a moment. "Did I detect an apology buried in there somewhere?"

"Yes," I said, "I think you did."

"All right," he nodded, "noted and accepted. I might have wondered too. Do you want in on the collar?"

"Nope, that's not what I came for. But I want a favor. When you check his house or whatever, keep an eye out for an old 30/06 rifle, possibly an army surplus Springfield, and some steel-jacketed ammo for it. You'll probably get a ballistics match for the slugs out at the Costa's hunting lodge. I think Hec used it for target practice the other day."

"Why would he do that?"

"Beats me," I said, "just a naturally destructive guy, I guess. Could be all that generic beer makes him crazy. You going to ask the state cops to send over a few hands for the harvest?"

"I don't think I'll trouble them about it, they've already had a long day. I think I'll buzz the National Guard unit over at Grayling and ask for a few people. They been dyin' to do their hitch in the war on drugs, maybe I'll give 'em a chance."

"Very generous of you. And since they can't take a piece of the collar, you'll save all that paperwork too."

"You know, I hadn't thought of that," he said innocently, "but I believe you're right. Sure you don't want a piece?"

"No thanks. My employers might not approve. They're not much on community involvement. Besides, I haven't eaten all day. I think I'll pop into Tubby's for a sandwich. Maybe I'll stop out later to see how it's going."

I spotted Rachel as soon as I came in the front door. She was wearing her oh-so-efficient black-and-white skirt and blouse ensemble. I think she noticed me too, because she promptly disappeared into the kitchen. I took my usual booth against the wall. The place was busy, but there was no sign of the Bush-hat party, and I said a silent prayer of thanks.

A tall, elderly gentleman dressed in white work clothes and wearing a red bow tie came out of the kitchen carrying a tray and walked briskly to my table. He carefully placed an aluminum foil-wrapped package in front of me.

"What's this?"

"Two venison steak sandwiches," he said, "to go."

"Look, about last night—"

"I don't care about last night," he interrupted, "I'm worried about today. So enjoy your lunch. Elsewhere."

"Could you tell Rachel Graham I'd like to talk to her? For just a minute?"

"It wouldn't do any good. She already told me to tell you goodbye, and she's the boss."

"The boss?"

"Yeah, she owns this place, and the motel, too. You didn't know that?"

"No, I didn't know. Are you the cook?"

"That's right. So?"

"You're an excellent cook," I said honestly.

"Thank you," he said. "And goodbye."

The harvest was in full swing when I pulled into the church parking lot. A half-dozen National Guardsmen in green fatigue uniforms were hacking industriously away in the cornfield and carrying the marijuana plants to a pile at the foot of the hill where LeClair and two Guard officers were conferring. I noticed Hec Michaud sitting disconsolately in a jeep, handcuffed to the steering wheel. I walked over.

"Hey meester," I said, "ju know where an hombre can find a chob pickin' beans?"

He just stared at the dashboard. No sense of humor.

"Hey, Flower! Come on up. I got bleacher seats and beer."

Paulie was sitting with his back against the toolshed on the hilltop, observing the proceedings. I trudged up the hill with my packet of sandwiches and eased down next to him. I unwrapped the tinfoil and passed him a sandwich. He handed me a can of generic beer.

"You arrange this little party too?" he asked.

"I helped a little," I said, taking a bite of my sandwich. It was absolutely delicious. "We still friends?"

"Sure," he said, surprised, "why shouldn't we be?"

"I just thought you might not be too happy about, well—having your life disrupted, you know?"

"You mean by gettin' ridda Hec? You gotta be kiddin'. He's been actin' weird ever since he planted the weed last spring."

"Paranoid, you mean?"

"Yeah, I guess that's right," he nodded, "paranoid."

"Did he ah, get a little paranoid the day the Costas were here?"

"Nah, he wasn't here that day. I told you that, didn't I?"

"Maybe. I guess I forgot."

"Was you wounded?" he said suddenly. "In 'Nam, I mean?"

"Yes."

"Where?"

"In the legs," I said, "and in the butt."

"In the ass," he nodded, "yeah, I guess that explains it."

"Explains what?"

"Why your memory's so bad," he grinned, and took a huge bite of his sandwich.

"Maybe so," I said, smiling with him. Last of the great interrogators. "Sorry if all this puts a crimp in your R&R."

"What, pullin' up the weed, you mean? Hell, I can't smoke that stuff, Flower. I got enough trouble keepin' track of things as it is. Hec just give me those joints so I'd keep my mouth shut about his stupid plants. Maybe I should have. I'm gonna be sorry to lose my job here."

"Whoever takes over Hec's job will still need a good worker, Paulie, you should be okay."

"I don't know," he said doubtfully, "some people just don't like me, you know? Like old lady Stansfield complainin' about me not wearin' a shirt that one time. What if the new guy don't like me neither? He might fire me, wouldn't he?"

"I suppose it's possible, Paulie, but I really don't think it'll go that way."

"Could you maybe help me out, Flower? Maybe talk to the new guy for me? Tell 'im how hard I work?"

"I'd be glad to, Paulie, but I probably won't be here. I'll be heading back to Detroit soon, maybe tomorrow morning."

"Yeah," he said, "that's right. You gotta go to Detroit. Well, can you maybe help out another way, then?"

"Sure, if I can. How?"

"Can you take the car back? Hec was gonna do it, but now . . ." He shrugged. "I don't know what to do about it now."

"What car?"

"That silver Lincoln, you know, that one the Costas had."

I turned slowly, staring at him. "What are you talking about?"

"The Costas' car," he said, irritated, "it's back in the trees there, across the field. It got stuck. Hec was gonna take it someplace and sell it, but then them other guys showed up askin' questions about it and he decided he better wait."

"When did this happen?" I asked, keeping my voice casual.

"When? I'm not sure. It was after the casket got stuck, though, I think. But I already told you about that, didn't I?"

"You told me the casket got stuck, but you didn't say anything about the car—"

"Yeah, but Hec said he'd fire me if I told that part. He was afraid people'd be all over the place and they'd find his patches. And then those guys showed up . . . I don't know what to do now."

"I want you to tell me the whole thing," I said carefully, "just take it slow, and we'll work through it. I can't help if I don't know what's going on, do you understand?"

"Can you help me keep my job?"

"I promise I'll help if I can, but one thing at a time, okay? Now, you said the casket got stuck, remember? What happened then?"

"Well, I didn't *see* it get stuck, you know? I was sacked out behind the toolshed when this Mr. Claudio wakes me up. He's havin' a heart attack because the box is jammed in the frame and everybody's gone but him and Mr. Costa. So I went down to take a look. I couldn't get it to move neither, but we got a crank in the shed to lower 'em manually so I came back up here to get it. On the way back I could hear Claudio and Mr. Costa arguin' clear across the cemetery. Then Claudio goes stompin' over to his hearse and drives off, which was strange, because the director's supposed to make sure everything's done before he leaves.

"Mr. Costa was standin' there lookin' at the coffin when I came up behind him. That's when I noticed the cloth. Charlie's million-dollar box had a little hunka red cloth stickin' out along the seam. Mr. Costa'd noticed it too, 'cause that's what he was starin' at. He spooked when I walked up, too.

"He told me to lower the box, and I said the funeral director's supposed to be here. 'Mr. Rigoni's been called away and I'll take full responsibility,' he says. 'You just lower it, and here's a little something for your trouble,' and he gives me two fifties. That's a lotta money, right?"

"Yes," I said, "it's a lot of money."

"I thought so too. I'm not very good with numbers any-more, but I figured there was something wrong, you know? So I said I couldn't lower it by myself, I'd need some help. He started to argue, and then he just turned and walked down to his car and tore out of the lot sprayin' gravel all over the place.

"I got down on my knees to take a closer look at the red cloth. And I swear to Christ it moved. Not much. Just a little. Like maybe somethin' was tryin' to pull it back inside the coffin. Scared the crap outa me."

"I can see where it would."

"Damn straight. I mean, I talk to stiffs sometimes to get a rise outa Hec, but this was for real, you know?

"But I was curious too, so I, ah, I rapped on the lid. Nothin' happened, of course, and I felt really stupid, and that ticked me off so I flipped the lugs and opened the damn thing up.

"She sat up and I sat down. Hard, man. A lady in a red dress, with blood on the side of her head, groggy, maybe blinded by the light. 'Help me,' she says. 'Help me.' "

"Is this the woman?" I asked, passing him the picture Mitch gave me.

He examined the photograph carefully, frowning. "Yeah, that's her. Who is she?"

"Charlie's girlfriend, Cindy Stanek."

"She was mumblin' something about Charlie," he nodded, "about talking or not talking, I don't know. She was in a daze like, you know? But then she musta come out of it a little, 'cause she looked down at who she was sittin' on. Her eyes kinda rolled up and she fell back down on Charlie. He didn't seem to mind."

"What happened then?"

"Well, I didn't know who she was, or what was goin' on, but I didn't figure she belonged in there with Charlie, so I hauled her out and shut the lid. But then I didn't know what to do. She needed help and there was nobody around. I didn't wanna leave her layin' there, so I picked her up and jogged all the way over to Mrs. Stansfield's house. The old lady doesn't like me much, but I couldn't think of anyplace else to go. Only nobody was home.

"I pounded on the damn door but nobody came and the house was locked. I was tired from the run, my head was hurting . . ."

He took a deep breath. "The girl—Cindy? Is that her name?"

I nodded.

"She was still out. I could see the dust of Costa's limo coming back and I knew I hadda do something, so I kicked the front door in, and set the girl inside. Then I ran back to the grave, keeping low. I didn't want Costa to know where I'd been. Besides, it was kinda fun anyway, like bein' back in the army.

"Mr. Costa'd brought his son back with him, Rollie Junior. Do you know Rollie?"

"I—know a little about him," I said, "enough to know he's bad news."

"Damn straight," Paulie said, "I used to see him at the beach sometimes in the summertime. Mean as a snake. Mr. Costa said he'd brought him along to help with the casket. I said okay, but he musta noticed I was still breathin' hard or somethin', 'cause he looks at me kinda funny and then he checked the box. I forgot to pop the lugs back down. So he opens it up again, and then he looks at me and his eyes were as dead as Charlie's. 'Where is she, boy?' he says, 'what've you done with her?'

"I tried playin' dumb, which ain't too hard for me. Don't know what you mean,' I say.

" 'Don't waste time on him,' Rollie says, 'he'll talk when he sees what his guts look like,' and he pulls this eight-inch blade. Man, that thing flicked open in his hand like magic."

"What did you do?"

"He wasn't no soldier," Paulie shrugged, "he was just a guy with a knife. My head don't work so good since the grenade got me and Gene, but I can still understand a guy with a knife. He came straight at me, big mistake. I snagged his knife wrist and spun him around into a chokehold, keeping him between me and his old man. Mr. Costa pulls this ugly little automatic, and then we all start shufflin' around, the old man tryna get a shot and me tryna keep Rollie in the middle. And then the girl screamed and Mr. Costa looked away. And that was an even bigger mistake." He took a long pull from his beer.

"What happened?" I asked quietly.

"I took 'em both down," he sighed, wincing at the memory, "I didn't know what else to do."

"Nothing," I said, "there was nothing else you could do. Where are they now, Paulie? Are they in the car?"

"The car? Nah, they're next to Charlie, under his monument stone. It hadn't been delivered yet, so I put 'em under the base. Figured it was the right place for 'em. The stone's too big for one guy anyway, but it's about right for three, and it says 'Costa' on it, right?"

"And the girl, Paulie? What about the girl?"

"She's still stayin' at Mrs. Stansfield's. I been over there a couple times to talk to her, but she's pretty weak and she can't say much. I guess she's glad to be out of that box, though."

"I imagine she is," I said, releasing a long, ragged breath I hadn't realized I'd been holding. "Paulie, we're going to have to tell Ira about this, you know."

"I wanted to in the first place, but Hec said I'd get in a lotta trouble. Am I gonna be in trouble now, Flower?"

"I don't know," I said, "maybe some. We'll see."

"One good thing at least, Mrs. Stansfield seems to like me a little better now. Maybe she was only grouchy before because she was lonely."

"Maybe so," I said, frowning. Something was nibbling at the back of my memory. "Paulie, didn't you tell me Mrs. Stansfield's house was west of the cemetery?"

He nodded, taking a pull at his beer.

I stared across the field of dry, snow-dusted cornstalks that stretched unbroken to the pine-covered hills on the horizon. The setting sun was hanging above them like a single milky eye. "Paulie, there is no house west of the cemetery."

"Sure there is," he said, with a trace of irritation, "that stone one just inside the fence there. Mrs. Stansfield's been here even longer'n the Major. Since 1852, I think, or maybe '51. I'm not very good at numbers anymore."

I stared at him a moment, speechless, too stunned to react, and then I was up and running, bounding across the face of the hill toward the old mausoleum, slipping and skidding in the snow, the icy air searing my throat. I stumbled over something and went down hard, driving the wind out of my aching ribs. I scrambled along on my hands and knees for a few yards before I managed to get up again and limp the rest of the way.

I yanked the rusty, wrought iron outer door open, banging it against the stone column that flanked the doorway with a clang that resounded through the tomb like a monstrous gong. The inner door appeared to be solid oak. I put my shoulder to it and it moved, but very slowly, as though someone was pushing against it from the inside.

And someone was.

But she didn't mean to be. And the heavy, fetid stench, and the rustle of tiny feet skittering away into the darkness told me I was too late. Too late by several weeks.

Chapter

Twenty-Two

LeClair didn't open the inner door. He ran his fingertips over the broken lock in the outer gate, shaking his head. "Gentle Jesus," he said softly, "he broke this damn thing clean in two. You've seen her? She's definitely in there?"

"She's in there," I said.

"And the other two are under the monument? My God, we were only a couple of feet away from them this morning. I, ah—" He swallowed hard, pinching the bridge of his nose with his gnarled fingertips. "Dammit," he said, taking a deep breath. "All right. First things first. Let's roll up this pissant drug bust and get the weekend warriors out of here. Schmitke won't want the area all stomped over. Don't say anything to anybody, meanwhile, and keep an eye on Paulie."

"I don't think that'll be necessary, he—"

"Just do it!" he said fiercely. He slammed the outer gate closed and stalked off through the snow.

"And then again," I said at his disappearing back, "I guess I could keep an eye on Paulie."

"What do you think will happen to him?" I asked.

"Who the hell knows," LeClair said, "nothing good, though, I can guarantee that." He was slumped in the passenger's seat of my rented Mustang. He looked utterly exhausted, but his eyes were bright, almost feverish. He was watching the men sitting in the back of the jeep ahead of us as we followed the small convoy back to Algoma in the thickening dusk. Paulie was talking animatedly with a couple of guardsmen, their smiles occasionally visible in my flickering headlights.

"Can you see him on the stand at the Coroner's inquest?" he said softly. "Christ, they'll have him for lunch. He'll go down to Ypsi for a three-month psycho evaluation, then back to the Vet's Facility if he's lucky, and maybe prison if he's not."

"He's got three bodies to explain," I said, "and I don't think he'll be very good at it."

"I understand he was mixed up in that scuffle at Tubby's last night. What happened there, anyway?"

"I think 'mixed up' is a little strong. He didn't start anything. I was getting my brains stomped in and he tried to help me. He didn't hurt anybody, although he's apparently capable of it."

"Yeah," LeClair said dryly, "apparently."

"My point is, he didn't hurt anybody, and he could have, that's all."

"You be sure to mention that at the inquest," he snapped, "I'm sure it'll impress the hell out of the prosecutor."

I didn't say anything.

"Sorry," he said after a moment, "it's not your fault. It's just that—ahhh, what a waste. What a goddamned waste."

"I don't like it any better than you do, but he killed two people, and at least contributed to the death of a third, and there's nothing either of us can do about it. It's out of our hands now."

"I suppose you're right," he said thoughtfully, "or at least it would be. If I considered you a credible witness."

"Meaning what?"

"Meaning I haven't actually seen any bodies, Cruz, all I know is what you told me. And I've already attended one grave-robbing party today on your say-so. And came up empty."

"There's a difference this time. I saw the girl's body."

"So you said," he agreed, "but on the other hand, I'm just a small-town sheriff and the Costas and Stansfields are rich, influential folks. I might be kinda reluctant to ask for, another exhumation on just your word. Or the word of a brain-damaged vet."

I glanced over at him. "You've got to be kidding."

"I don't know if I am or not. I'll give it to you straight. I don't give a damn about what happened to the Costas, I'm just sorry it happened here. It's tough about the girl, but she should have been choosier about her playmates and there's no helping her now. That only leaves Paulie. He's already been ground up in the machinery once, and I'll be god-damned if I'll be the one to feed him back into the hopper again."

"Three people are dead," I said.

"You're wrong, sport, a lot more people are dead than that. My boy was one of 'em. He got blown to hell in some Vietnamese hole while Rollie Costa was learning the family rackets and shootin' up the woods with his goddamn legal tommy guns."

"Unh-uh," I said, "no chance. Look, I feel lousy about Paulie too, but concealing evidence in a homicide is a felony. You have no right to ask me to do something like that."

"I'm not asking you anything, Cruz. I'm just telling you what I'm gonna do. Nothing. Nada. I'm dumpin' it on you. You decide who owes who what and let me know, okay?"

"That's not fair," I said flatly.

"No kidding?" he said, stifling a yawn. "Well, I'm used to

things that aren't fair. I'm the law. And don't worry about Hec. I can handle him."

"Look, I'm sorry," I said, "but there's no way I'm getting involved in this. We'd never get away with it."

"I think we can," he said, "but if not at least I'm covered. I'll just scuff my toe in the dirt and say I was taken in by a smooth-talkin' slick from the big city. I don't know what your excuse'd be, but that's your problem."

I didn't say anything for awhile. I thought I heard the faint sound of laughter from the jeep ahead drift past on the wind, but it was probably my imagination. I glimpsed the streetlights of the village glowing in the distance through the gently falling snow. Both of them. Home for the Holidays. Terrific.

"It's just not that simple," I said, "Roland's people won't stop looking for them. They think they're a threat."

"The people who hired you, you mean?"

"The people who hired me," I acknowledged.

"Good," he said, "handling them is your headache. So how about it, Cruz? You up to it?"

"What the hell," I sighed. "I guess I can always plead insanity."

"Sure you can. And I'll back you a hundred percent on that."

"Thank you," I said, "thank you very much."

Chapter

Twenty-Three

I rapped gently on Lugo's door, and a moment later it opened the width of the chain.

"It's me," I said, "we need to talk."

He was wearing a maroon velvet robe with black piping over navy and green striped pajamas and black velvet slippers. And somehow it all seemed to blend on him. His dark hair was tousled, but he seemed alert and wary. As usual.

"Wanna beer?" he asked, flopping back on the bed amid the wreckage of the sports section. A tape of three Oriental women doing complicated things to each other on a gym set was playing on his new VCR. I walked over and turned it off. He raised his eyebrows.

"This better be good," he said, taking a bottle of Heineken from the cooler by the bed.

"I think you'll like it," I said, easing down into the room's only chair. And I told him. Everything. He listened without comment, sipping his ale. He only interrupted me once, when I mentioned the girl being in the casket alive.

"That's got style," he said, nodding in approval, "I bet that was Rollie's idea. Always did have a flair for that kinda stuff."

"Maybe it had style," I said, "but it wasn't too bright."

"Right. Rollie all the way. Tell me the rest."

And I did. Including what LeClair had suggested on the way back. He didn't say anything when I finished. He took a cigarillo from a platinum case on the nightstand, bit off the end and spat it on the carpet, and lit up.

"All right," he nodded, "I think we're in good shape here. Keepin' the lid on'll suit Bradleigh just fine. He likes things quiet. One part I don't get. Why's the local law wanna keep this cool? Is the gravedigger a relative or what?"

"Not that I know of."

"So what's it to him if the guy goes in the joint?"

"I don't know. I guess he feels responsible for him."

He examined the glowing tip of his cigar thoughtfully, as though he was reading the future in it. And maybe he was. "Good," he said at last, "even that part works out. There won't be no fuss later if somethin's gotta be done."

"What do you mean?"

"About the gravedigger," he said, surprised. "He took out two of our people. I don't think the ol' man'll let that pass. Too messy. He'll probably wanna make things right."

"No," I said, "he can't do that."

"He can't? Why not?"

"Because it's over now. Finished. But if anything happens to Paulie, you're going to have a whole new set of problems."

"What kinda problems? With some hick-town sheriff?"

"No. With me. You're going to have problems with me."

"With you," he echoed, smiling. "No kiddin'? Why? This guy a friend of yours?"

"Yes. I guess he is, in a way."

"How long you known him, this friend?"

"It doesn't matter. Just let him alone. He's got no part in this."

"Wrong, he dealt himself in. You're the one ain't got no parta this now, Cruz. Look, you done good here. You turned 'em up when nobody figured you would. So walk away. You're out of it. Hell, I'll get Bradleigh to give ya a bonus."

"No," I said, "I guess I can't do that. Let him alone."

"You know, you're doin' me a helluva favor here, Cruz. I tell Tio Eladio you say we gotta lay off whatsisname, he's gonna make me a package deal to whack the botha ya just for messin' with us."

"Whatever," I said, getting up. "You do what you have to. Right now I'm too tired to care. The sheriff said he'll leave the Lincoln at the beach house tomorrow with the keys in the glove compartment. I'm pulling out tonight. I'd say it's been fun working with you, Lugo, but it hasn't. I hope I won't see you again."

"I think you will," he said. "Motown's not so big if you're tryin' to hide. Hey, Cruz?"

I paused in the doorway.

"You said I was stupid before. Well you're the one who's stupid, mixin' in this when you don't have to. Really stupid."

"No argument from me," I said, "I think you're absolutely right."

Chapter

Twenty-Four

Cordell picked me up at the American Airlines entrance at Detroit Metro in his mint '75 Volkswagen bus. The bus is a lot like him, long and lean, and resourceful, and he can park it on the Corridor without worrying about finding it stripped. Most of the punks leave it alone because they know whose it is, and the rest leave it alone because there's no market for the parts. I tossed my bags in the back and climbed up into the passenger's seat. He was wearing faded Levi's, a black turtleneck, and a bombardier jacket, and still managed to look very well dressed. A puzzlement. Cordell was the only guy I ever knew who looked elegant in jungle fatigues.

Neither of us spoke until we were clear of the airport confusion, headed east on I-94 into the city.

"You're back early," he said, "you can't handle fresh air anymore?"

"Something like that," I said, and I told him the whole thing, quickly and without embellishment. He nodded at the proper intervals, but otherwise made no comment at all.

"Well?" I said, "so what do you think?"

"For openers, I think I won't say I told you so. It'd be tacky."

"You're right, it would. I appreciate that."

"No charge. How much time before they move, assumin' they're goin' to?"

"I don't know. A few days, a week. Soon, I think."

"So how you wanna work it, Bobby? You want to take a vacation, see if this thing cools? You want me to talk to 'em? What?" He swerved the Volks into the passing lane, gunning past a pair of semis running abreast.

"I just took a vacation," I said, "it wasn't so hot. And I don't see any point in talking to them. Their credibility quotient would be zilch anyway."

"Sad but true," Cordell nodded. "Well, I'd run out on you in a second, but I can't cut any courses right now without screwin' up my grade-point, which brings us back to square one."

"How much is in the kitty?" I said.

"Five grand and change, and we're up to date on everything."

"Then how about taking some basic precautions, cyclone screen the front windows, replace both doors with steel, put in an alarm system. We could do most of it ourselves and finish in a couple of days."

"Maybe," he said, "and then what?"

"There's an empty apartment in my building I can probably stay in temporarily. Other than that we keep our heads up and it's business as usual."

He didn't say anything for a mile or two, mulling it over. Then he shook his head. "Doin' the office is okay, but it's not really the problem, you know. The street's the problem. Too many people. If they put a contract on the street, eventually somebody's gonna get a crack at you. Or us."

"I don't think they'll do that."

"No? Why not?"

"A hunch. I think Lugo'll want to do me himself."

"You willin' to bet your life on this hunch? 'Cause that's what you're doin'.'"

"You proposing any alternatives?"

"Other'n doin' a rabbit, you mean? Not a one. Except, if we're gonna spend some bucks on security for the office, how about we fix it up a little while we're at it? I did a collection for a dude does carpenter work awhile back. I think he'd make us a deal."

"Go out in style, you mean?"

"Why not?"

"Right. Why not."

"You know they, ah, they got this insurance for partner-ships that pays off if one partner dies. I don't suppose . . . ?"

"Forget it," I said.

"You're an inconsiderate man, Bobby," Cordell sighed, shaking his head, "you always were."

I told Cordell I expected something to happen soon, but of course soon is a relative term. The carpenters were in and out in three days. They replaced the doors and the paneling and painted the trim; Cordell and I installed an alarm system, and then things were back to business as usual. Almost.

I began parking my battered Camaro in front of the office in view of the window, and checking it over before cranking it up. I kept my arrivals and departures inconsistent, not that that was much of a change, and I always looked the street over before leaving the office or my apartment. But Cordell was right, there was really no way to defend the Corridor.

Street people are around and about Cass Avenue twenty-four hours a day, drifters and derelicts, hookers lounging around the bus stops. Crack dealers work out of the aban-doned HUD houses on the side streets or hawk crack openly near the Wayne State campus. I've always liked the action on the street, the raw energy of it. It's one reason we located here, plus the rockbottom rent and the nearby campus. But now it was a threat. If the Delagarza people contracted the hit out on me, I had a real problem. And when it came down to it, all I had going for me was a gut feeling. A hunch.

And I was wrong.

I was alone in the office on Friday afternoon when the cream-colored Mercedes stretch limo pulled up to the curb. I half-expected an army, but Cobb, the gopher/bodyguard, was the only one who got out. And he was alone. I glassed the Benz through the office window to make sure while he was fumbling at the front door.

And then I buzzed him through.

He looked prosperous. And nervous. He was wearing a cashmere overcoat over a dark suit, a red striped tie, Nunn Bush jodhpurs and a Homburg. He looked like a trade rep for the Warsaw Pact.

"Cruz," he nodded, "you got a minute?"

"Sure. Have a seat." Neither of us offered to shake hands.

"I guess you figured we forgot about you."

"Not at all," I said, "I thought you'd get around to me eventually. Look, let's get to it. What do you want?"

He reached inside his overcoat, and paused, his eyes widening as he stared down the barrel of my Model 92. My speed probably wouldn't have impressed Randolph Scott, but it seemed to work pretty well on Cobb. I'd been practicing.

"Hey," he said, "what is this?"

"You tell me. You're the one with his hand in his coat."

"It's just a letter."

"Next time use the mail. Show it to me. Slowly. And that's all I'd better see."

"Sure, sure, just cool it, okay?" He extracted a business-sized manila envelope from his lapel pocket, and held it in the air in his fingertips. "See? Okay?"

"Toss it here and put both your hands flat on the desk."

"Look, there's—"

"Just do it," I said mildly, cocking the hammer back.

"Okay, okay, don't get excited."

I placed the cocked Beretta on the desk in front of me and opened the envelope. There was no note. Just a check from Bradleigh, Childreth and Osbourne. For ten thousand dollars.

"What the hell is this?" I said.

"It's your end."

"My end of what?"

"You know, for that—situation up north there. For doing the right thing."

"What are you talking about?"

He glanced around uneasily.

"It's all right," I said, "we can talk. So start."

"Look, Lugo said you helped him—you know, clean up the mess up there, by, ah, takin' the girl out while he handled the Costas. So this is your end. Ten grand a head was the deal."

I stared at him a moment, too surprised to say anything. Then I bounced the envelope off his chest. "I'm not taking this."

"Ah, crap," he said, exasperated, "Lugo said I might have problems with you. Look, you might as well take it because it's the best deal you're gonna get. You wanna negotiate you'll hafta wait till next time. You ain't got a lotta leverage on this one, since the job's done already. You send this back and it's like you throw it in the old man's face. You might as well pick up your piece there and blow your fuckin' brains out with it, save us the trouble of sendin' somebody around, you know? Besides, I don't see where you got no beef. You wasn't hired for the wet work in the first place. I don't know what you usually get for this kinda thing, but from the looksa this place it can't be all that much, so just take the money, okay? Don't make waves."

I picked up the check, then tossed it back on the desk.

"All right," I nodded, "I guess I don't have much choice. But you tell Bradleigh I won't work for him again, understand?"

"Jesus, nobody's askin' ya to. It was a one-time thing and seems to me you came out way ahead, so don't get all swole up with yourself. You ain't exactly our speed, you know?"

"That's some comfort. Will you see Lugo?"

"I'll probably see him around," he said cautiously, "why?"

"Tell him I said *gracias*."

"Thanks? That's a little more like it."

"Not thanks. *Gracias*. There's a difference. Not to me. To him. Make sure you get it right. Now take a hike."

I picked up the check again and examined it after he'd gone. It was all very proper and businesslike, made out to Mr. Roberto A. Cruz, Alma Investigations. The memo line read 'for services rendered.'

Services rendered. Interesting phrase. Burial services maybe?

It didn't matter. It was a better deal than I had any right to expect. Lugo'd done me a favor in order to do himself a bigger one. Ten thousand to insure my discretion while he collected the other twenty. I'd underestimated him, and instead of getting killed for it, I'd been paid for killing somebody else. Hell, I'd even underestimated his sense of humor.

Still, I guess I can live with that, considering the alternatives. The only problem I see is that Lugo will probably figure

I owe him a big one, and maybe he's right.

I decided to close the office early, pick up Cordell after class, and treat us to a long, liquid lunch. Maybe the *Pegasus* in Greektown. Moussaka, steamed squash, baklava with cinnamon. And ouzo, of course, lots of ouzo. After all we had things to celebrate. And things to discuss. New carpeting? Or maybe an answering machine.

And whether he's absolutely sure we're in the right end of the business.

FICTION
Allyn, Douglas.
Welcome to wolf country